COUNT VALIERI'S
PRISONER

COUNT VALIERI'S PRISONER

BY

SARA CRAVEN

MILLS & BOON

First published in Great Britain 2013
by Mills & Boon, an imprint of Harlequin (UK) Limited.
Large Print edition 2013
Harlequin (UK) Limited, Eton House,
18-24 Paradise Road, Richmond, Surrey TW9 1SR

© Sara Craven 2013

ISBN: 978 0 263 23210 3

Printed and bound in Great Britain
by CPI Antony Rowe, Chippenham, Wiltshire

CHAPTER ONE

IT WAS QUIET in the lamplit room, the only sound the occasional rustle of paper as the man seated on one side of the vast antique desk went through the contents of the file in front of him. He was unhurried, his black brows drawn together in a faint frown as he closely scanned each printed sheet in turn, then laid it aside.

The grey-haired man sitting opposite watched him, under the guise of studying his fingernails. It was over two years since they'd had cause to meet face to face, and there was no longer even a trace of the boy he had once known in the dark, incisive face bent over the documents he had brought for him only a few hours ago.

He had been welcomed with the usual courtesy, conducted by the *maggiodomo* to the room where he would spend the night, after which he had dined alone with his host. The food had been delicious, and on the surface, it was all charm and relaxation, but he was under no illusions.

The real business of his visit was being conducted right here and now.

Eventually, his reading concluded, the younger man looked up and gave a brief nod of approbation.

'You have been more than thorough, Signor Massimo. I commend you. An entire life laid out for my inspection in every detail. Invaluable.'

His swift smile momentarily softened the hard lines of his mouth and brought an added glint to eyes that were almost the colour of amber, flecked with gold.

It was a proud face with a high-bridged nose, classically moulded cheekbones and an uncompromising chin.

But now too austere to be truly handsome, thought Guido Massimo as he inclined his head in polite acknowledgement. And too coldly purposeful. The face of a stranger.

He waited as the other took the photograph which was the last object remaining in the file and studied it. The girl looking back at him was blonde, her pale hair hanging in a sleek silken curtain almost to her shoulders. Her face was oval with creamy skin, her eyes a clear grey. Her nose was short and straight, her chin firm and the delicately curved lips were parted in a slight but confident smile.

'When was this taken?'

'A few months ago on the occasion of her engagement,' Signor Massimo returned. 'It appeared in a magazine published in the county where she was brought up.' He allowed himself a discreet twinkle. *'Che bella ragazza.'*

His comment received only an indifferent shrug.

'This cool Anglo-Saxon type has no appeal for me.' The other's mouth twisted. 'Which, under the circumstances, must be deemed fortunate.' He paused. 'But no doubt her *fidanzato* will have a very different view and will pay the required price for her safe return. Or we must hope so.'

Signor Massimo murmured politely, keeping his expression impassive. He was well aware that his host's tastes in women favoured the elegantly voluptuous, but it would have been unwise even to hint that he possessed such knowledge.

The younger man returned the photograph to the file with an air of finality and leaned back in his chair, frowning again. 'The wedding is scheduled to take place in two months, which means there is no time to be lost. However it will make the resolution of the matter increasingly urgent, which is all to the good.'

Almost absently he began to play with the heavy gold signet ring he wore on his right hand. 'Tell me more about this television company she works for. You say it makes programmes for various arts channels?'

'And with some success. She is currently a researcher with a desire to move into production, but it seems marriage will end such hopes. As I have mentioned in the report, her *fidanzato* has already made it clear that he does not want his wife to work.'

The other nodded. 'And this has a caused—a certain amount of friction?'

'It seems so. As yet unresolved.'

'Ambition versus love.' The cool, deep voice spoke more softly. Became almost meditative. 'Which will she choose, I wonder, when serious temptation is offered.' He paused. 'Are you a betting man, Signor Massimo?'

'On rare occasions only.'

'And where would you place your money in such a situation.'

Guido Massimo gave a faint shrug. 'A girl soon to be a bride. She will wish to please her groom, I think.'

'You are unexpectedly romantic, *signore*. But I feel you are mistaken.' His smile was a curl of the lips. 'Because I know the bait that will bring her to me.'

'If I can be of further assistance...' the older man began, but was stopped by a raised hand.

'I am grateful but I believe that from here it is better for your involvement to cease. What happens should be my responsibility, and I would not wish you to have to answer any awkward questions, so the less you know the better.'

His tone became brisker. 'Leaving just the matter of your fee to be dealt with.' He opened a drawer in the desk, extracted a bulky envelope and handed it over. 'For the same reasons, we agreed this transaction should be on a cash basis. You may of course count it.'

'I would not dream of such a thing.'

'As you please.' The other paused. 'Which means I have only to thank you once more and wish you a peaceful night. We shall meet tomorrow at breakfast.'

Guido Massimo rose, made a slight bow and walked to the door where he hesitated. 'I must ask this. You are—determined? Quite sure there is no other course? The girl, after all, is an innocent party in all this. Does she deserve to be treated in such a way? I only enquire, you understand.'

'I comprehend perfectly. But you must not distress yourself, my friend. Once I have what I want, your *bella ragazza* will be returned as good as new to her future husband.' He added unsmilingly, 'That is, of course, if she still wants him.' He rose too, tall and lithe, his hands resting on his lean hips. 'There is no necessity to pity her, I assure you.'

But I shall do so, just the same, Guido Massimo thought as he left the room. And I shall also pity the boy I once knew, and remember him in my prayers.

'Darling,' said Jeremy. 'Please tell me this is some sort of joke.'

Madeleine Lang put down her glass and stared at him across the table in the wine bar in genuine perplexity. 'A joke?' she repeated. 'I'm talking about work here and perfectly serious. Why on earth would I be joking?'

Jeremy gave a hollow laugh. 'Oh, just a small matter of a wedding for over two hundred guests to arrange. Or will that be put on hold while you roam round Italy on some wild goose chase?'

Madeleine bit her lip. 'Hardly on hold, with your stepmother so firmly in control. I doubt if my absence will even be noticed.'

There was an edgy pause, then Jeremy reached across and took her hand, his expression rueful.

'Sweetheart, I know Esme can be rather managing...'

Madeleine sighed. 'Jeremy, that's putting it mildly, and you know it. Everything I want and suggest is just—brushed aside. I don't even feel that it is our wedding any more.'

'I'm sorry, Maddie.' Jeremy's tone was coaxing. 'But—it's a really big deal for the family, and Dad wants everything to be perfect. Times may be hard but Sylvester and Co is still riding high. That kind of thing.'

'If it only was a family affair,' Madeleine muttered. She sat back, reaching for her glass. 'For one thing, where have all those guests come from? I've never even heard of two thirds of them.'

'Clients of the bank, business associates, old friends of my father.' Jeremy sounded rueful. 'But believe me it could have been very much worse. What we have now is the shortlist.'

'I don't find that particularly reassuring,' Madeleine told him candidly.

'Oh, come on, it's not that bad.' Jeremy paused awkwardly. 'But it could be if you persist with this Italian nonsense.'

She said slowly, 'I can't believe you just said that. First it was a joke, now it's nonsense. Jeremy, we're talking about my work here...'

'It used to be your work.' His tone was defensive. 'But very soon now it won't be, so what is the point in your shooting off across Europe in pursuit of some musician no-one's ever heard of?'

'But people have heard of her,' Madeleine fired back. 'Floria Bartrando was said to be the most wonderful young soprano of her generation. It was predicted she was going to be another Maria Callas, and then suddenly, with no explanation, she dropped off the edge of the world. It's been a major mystery for thirty years and now I have the chance to solve it.'

'But why you?' Frowning, he refilled their glasses. 'You're not the only researcher on the team.'

'Apparently the Italian contacts saw the programme on Hadley Cunningham's last symphony,' Madeleine said levelly. 'The one no-one knew he'd written. I did most of the research on that. So Todd offered me this.'

Jeremy's frown deepened. 'Frankly, darling, when you said you had something to tell me I assumed you meant that you'd handed in your notice as we'd agreed.'

'I said I'd think about it,' Madeleine said quietly. 'Having done so, I'm not walking away from a job

I love without good reason.' She added, 'But I have booked out our honeymoon weeks as holiday.'

Jeremy stared at her as if she'd grown an extra head. 'And I'm supposed to be grateful for that?' he asked sarcastically.

'Well, you should be,' she said cheerfully. 'After all, you'd hardly want to go to the Maldives on your own.'

'I'm sorry, but I don't find this particularly amusing.'

'And nor do I. In fact I'm perfectly serious.' She gave him a rueful look. 'Jeremy, please try to understand.'

'What's to understand?' His shrug was almost petulant. 'Clearly finding material for minority interest television channels matters more to you than being my wife.'

'And now you're talking nonsense,' Madeleine retorted hotly. 'It's the twenty-first century, for heaven's sake, and most women combine marriage and a career these days in case you hadn't noticed.'

'Well, I want you to regard our marriage as your career,' Jeremy said, his lips tightening. 'I don't think you appreciate how hectic our social life will become, or how much entertaining we'll have to do. And I mean full blown dinner parties, not you rushing in at the last moment with a takeaway.'

She gasped. 'Is that how you see me? As some ditsy incompetent?'

'No, my sweet, of course not.' He was back in placatory mode. 'It's just that we're not sure you realise how much you'll be taking on, or how stressful you might find it.'

Maddie sat back in her seat, and gave him a straight look. 'I presume that's not the royal "we" you were using there? That you're quoting your father?'

'Naturally it's been discussed.'

She bit her lip. 'Jeremy—the wedding may have got away from us, but this is our marriage, and you must make him see that.' Her voice deepened in intensity. 'I have no intention of letting you down, or failing to provide you with the support you need in your career. All I ask is that you do the same for me. Is that so very hard?'

There was a silence, then he said, 'I suppose—not when you put it like that. I'll talk to Dad again. Which reminds me...' He glanced at his watch and pulled a face. 'I should be going. I'm due to meet him with some people at The Ivy.'

He paused. 'Sure you won't come with me? It's no problem.'

Maddie got to her feet, forcing a smile as she indicated the slim-fitting jeans and white shirt she was wearing. 'Except I'm not dressed for dinner at a top restaurant, which might create its own difficulty. Another time, darling.'

'So what will you do?' He sounded anxious.

She shrugged on her navy and white checked jacket and reached for her canvas shoulder bag. 'Oh—have a girlie night in, washing my hair, giving myself a manicure.'

And I have just told my fiancé, the man I love, my first deliberate lie. Because actually, I'm going back to the office to do some more work on Floria Bartrando, but I doubt it would be politic to say so at this juncture.

Jeremy pulled her to him and kissed her. 'We mustn't fight,' he muttered. 'We can work things out. I know it.'

'Yes,' she said. 'Of course we can.' And kissed him back.

Outside the wine bar, she watched him hail a cab, then waved goodbye before beginning to walk slowly back towards the street where the Athene television production company was based.

She supposed that the recent confrontation had been inevitable, but knowing that made it no easier to handle. Somehow, she had to convince Jeremy that she could succeed as a working wife, a task handicapped from the outset by his father's forthright and openly expressed opinions to the contrary.

Maddie had known the Sylvesters pretty much all her life. Beth Sylvester, an old school friend of her mother, had been her godmother, and, as a child, Maddie had spent part of every summer at Fallowdene, the Sylvesters' big country house.

It had always seemed idyllic to her, but in retrospect she could see there'd been undercurrents which she'd been too young to pick up.

But somehow she'd known instinctively from the first that while her godmother would always be 'Aunt Beth', her husband would remain 'Mr Sylvester' and never become 'Uncle Nigel'.

Fallowdene was not in itself a beautiful house, yet to Maddie it had always seemed an enchanted place, especially when Jeremy, the Sylvesters' only son, seven years her senior and light years older in every way, was there to be shadowed adoringly.

But she'd never allowed him to get away with any implication that they'd been childhood sweethearts.

'Arrant nonsense,' she'd teased, the first time it was mentioned. 'You thought I was a total pain in the neck, and went out of your way to ignore me.'

'But I've made up for it since,' he'd whispered, drawing her close. 'Admit it.'

Yet her most abiding memories were not of Jeremy at all, even though her initial crush had lasted well into her early teens.

What she recalled very vividly was the way the atmosphere of the house underwent a subtle change when Nigel Sylvester came home.

He was a man of just above medium height, who somehow gave the impression of being much taller. He had gone prematurely grey in his late twenties, or so Jeremy had told her, adding glumly, 'I hope it doesn't happen to me.'

Maddie had stroked his cheek, smiling. 'You'd look extremely distinguished.'

But if she was totally honest, she'd always found Nigel Sylvester's silver hair, which he wore slightly longer than was fashionable and swept straight back from his forehead, to be in odd and disturbing contrast to his curiously smooth, unlined face, and dark brown heavy-lidded eyes.

Nor was it just his appearance that used to unnerve her. His standards were exacting, he missed nothing, and although she had never heard him raise his voice in displeasure, Maddie often thought it would have been better if he had shouted occasionally.

Because, there was something about his quietness which dried Maddie's throat when he spoke to her, and made her stumble over her words. Not that she ever had too much to say to him. She'd divined fairly soon that her presence at Fallowdene was tolerated by him, rather than welcomed, and tried to keep out of his way.

It wasn't too difficult. She'd been given the old nursery as her room, and this contained a glass-fronted bookcase, crammed with children's books by well-known authors in a range that appealed from tots to teens.

At first, when she was very young, Aunt Beth had read them as bedtime stories. Later, she'd been happy to while away solitary hours in their company.

But her happy childhood had been brought to an abrupt and tragic end one terrible winter night when an icy road and a driver who'd drunk too much at an office party had fatally combined to take both her parents from her.

She'd been staying with Aunt Fee, her mother's younger sister, at the time, and her aunt had immediately assumed charge of her, only to be approached after the funeral by Aunt Beth with an offer to adopt her god-daughter.

But the offer had been refused. Instead Aunt Fee and Uncle Patrick, her big genial husband had been quietly adamant that Maddie belonged with them, and she'd been loved, allowed to grieve then eventually find healing in their comfortable untidy house.

Her visits to Fallowdene, however, continued as before, although the question of adoption was never raised again and, in hindsight, Maddie was sure that Nigel Sylvester had probably opposed the idea from the outset.

She realized since that, although she'd been too young to recognize it at the time, he had represented her first brush with real power.

And she'd often wondered what had persuaded her godmother, with her quiet prettiness and sudden mischievous, enchanting smile, to marry him.

She had been in her first year at university when Aunt Beth died very suddenly in her sleep of a heart attack. She'd attended the funeral with her aunt and uncle and haltingly attempted to express her sorrow to Mr Sylvester, who'd muttered an abrupt word of thanks, then turned away.

And she was realistic enough to know that she would no longer be welcome at Fallowdene.

A week or so later she was astonished to receive a letter from a law firm informing her that Aunt Beth had left her a sum of money substantial enough to get her through her degree course without having to seek a student loan, with an additional bequest of the entire book collection from the nursery, which somehow meant far more than the money.

'Oh, how wonderful of her,' she'd said softly, wiping her eyes. 'She always knew how much I loved them.' She paused. 'But won't Jeremy want them?'

'It seems not,' Aunt Fee said rather drily. 'I gather if you'd refused the bequest they'd have gone to a charity shop.' She pursed her lips. 'No doubt they reminded Nigel too much of the wonderful career he'd interrupted.'

'Career?' Maddie repeated. 'Was she a writer once?' She frowned. 'She never told me.'

'No, that wasn't her talent. She was a very successful editor with Penlaggan Press. She found the authors of all those books, encouraged them, and published them.

'Your mother told me Penlaggan did their best to coax her back on numerous occasions, even offering to let her work from home.' She shook her head. 'But it never happened. Sylvester wives, it seems, do not work.'

'But if she was so good at her job…'

'That,' said Aunt Fee somberly, 'was probably the trouble.'

It was an insight into Aunt Beth's marriage that

Maddie had never forgotten. And now it had a renewed and unpleasing resonance.

Well, I'm good at my job too, she thought, and I'm damned if I'm giving it up whatever Jeremy or his father may say about it.

She still felt raw when she remembered how Nigel Sylvester, having mourned for barely a year, announced his engagement to a widow called Esme Hammond and married her only a month later.

But then, quite unexpectedly, she'd met Jeremy again at a party in London. He'd expressed delight at seeing her and asked for her phone number, but if she felt this was more out of politeness than serious intent, she soon discovered she was wrong. Because he'd not only called but invited her to dinner. After which, events had seemed to snowball, she remembered, smiling.

Jeremy had changed a great deal from the taciturn, aloof boy who'd so consistently avoided an annoying small girl. He seemed to have inherited much of his mother's charm, but in spite of three years at university and a spell at the Harvard Business School before joining Sylvester and Co, he still seemed under his father's thumb.

But while Maddie did not delude herself she would have been his daughter-in-law of choice, at least Nigel Sylvester had not openly opposed the engagement.

But she still didn't call him 'Uncle Nigel', she thought, pausing at the office's street entrance to punch in her entry code. Nor, after the wedding, would he ever morph into 'Dad', 'Pa' or 'Pops'.

And he had put a spoke in their wheel in another way.

If Maddie had assumed that Jeremy would immediately want her to move into the company flat with him, she soon found she was wrong..

'Dad says he needs to use the flat himself on occasion,' he told her. 'And it would make things— awkward if you were there. And anyway he feels we should wait to live together until we're actually married.'

Maddie had stared at him. 'But who on earth does that nowadays?'

Jeremy shrugged. 'I guess he's just old-fashioned about these things.'

But Maddie was convinced 'hypocritical' was a better description, and would have wagered a year's salary that his father and the glamorous Esme had been sharing a bed even while Aunt Beth was alive.

'And what happens after the wedding?' she asked. 'Because, we'll be living there then, or will your father expect me to move out any time he plans to stay overnight?'

'No, of course not,' he said impatiently. 'He's talking of taking a suite at a hotel.' He pulled a face. 'And, believe me, sweetie, it could be worse. When it began, Sylvester and Co was Sylvester, Felderstein and Marchetti. You could be having all sorts of foreign directors dropping in.'

'Might have been fun,' Maddie said lightly. 'So why aren't there any now?'

Jeremy shrugged again. 'The families died out, or started new ventures of their own. That's what Dad said, anyway. We only became fully independent in my grandfather's day.'

Since when Nigel Sylvester had achieved success in the corridors of power, joining various government think-tanks and advising on banking and economic affairs.

So much so that, rumour had it that he would be offered a life peerage in the next New Year Honours' List.

I wonder if he'll expect me to call him 'My lord' she mused as she took the creaky elevator to her office on the first floor. *Or curtsy when we meet. While Esme will be even more insufferable when she's Lady Sylvester.*

But I'll deal with that when I have to, she told

herself. For now, I'm concentrating on this dream assignment that's come my way.

Italy in May, she thought with an ecstatic sigh. Boy, I can hardly wait.

CHAPTER TWO

IT WASN'T UNTIL the plane had taken off that Maddie really believed she was going to Italy.

In view of the events of the past ten days, she would hardly have been surprised if Nigel Sylvester had found some way to have her bodily removed from the aircraft.

It had all come to a head over dinner at the company flat. She had believed with pleasurable anticipation that she and Jeremy would be alone, and was shaken to find his father and Esme waiting for her too, with Mr Sylvester telling her, with his thin-lipped smile, 'We feel we should all get to know each other a little better, Madeleine.'

Heart sinking, as she realised Jeremy was avoiding her gaze, she'd replied, 'By all means,' and accepted the dry sherry she was offered.

Conversation had been light and general over dinner, but she'd only picked at the excellent meal, cooked by the housekeeper Mrs Palmer, and watched with trepidation as the good woman was thanked and dismissed once the coffee and brandy were on the table.

The door had barely closed behind her when Esme leaned forward. 'I think, Madeleine, if the men will forgive us boring them with feminine affairs, we need to discuss your wedding dress as a matter of urgency.'

Maddie put down her coffee cup, bewildered. 'But that's all in hand.'

Mrs Sylvester's arched brows lifted. 'Indeed? I am not sure I understand.'

'I've chosen my dress and it's already being made by Janet Gladstone, who owns the bridal shop in the village. You must have seen it.'

'Not that I recall.' Esme's tone suggested she had not noticed the High Street either. 'And, anyway, I've made an appointment for you with Nina Fitz-Alan in three days' time.' Her smile was complacent. 'As I'm a favoured client she has agreed to drop everything in order to supply us with a gown of her own exclusive design. But there is no time to be lost.'

'That's very kind of you,' Maddie said evenly. 'But I'm afraid I can't possibly alter my arrangements, especially as Aunt Fee and Uncle Patrick are paying for my dress, and those of the bridesmaids.'

'And naturally you feel that a top London designer is beyond their reach, financially.' The older woman nodded. 'Well, don't concern yourself about that. Nina's bill, of course, will be sent to me. There is no need for your aunt and uncle to be bothered.'

'But they will be bothered. And so will I. Very much so.' Maddie ignored Jeremy's pleading glance from the other side of the table. 'Because I'm getting exactly what I want. White wild silk embroidered with silver flowers. I've already had two fittings, and it's going to be beautiful.'

Esme allowed herself the small, tinkling laugh that made Maddie's teeth ache. 'I don't think you have quite grasped, my dear, that you are dressing for a very important occasion. And a village-made frock, however pretty, just will not do.'

She paused. 'So we will have a preliminary meeting with Nina at ten thirty on Thursday, after which you will hold yourself available for fittings at her salon whenever required.

'And as you've mentioned bridesmaids,' she went on. 'Perhaps this is the time to say that while I admire your loyalty in wanting your flatmates Sally and—Tracey, is it…'

'Trisha,' said Maddie.

'I think I told you.' Esme swept on, 'that Nigel

would like his godsons' little ones to be your attendants. Two pigeon pairs—so convenient—and, I thought, in Victorian dress. Those charming caps for the boys, and frilly pantaloons for the little girls.'

Maddie's hands were clenched tightly in her lap. 'And I think I made it clear that I would not, under any circumstances, have very small children following me up the aisle. Especially ones I have never met, but, I gather, are barely potty-trained. Which,' she added, 'would make me fear for the pantaloons. Besides, Sally and Trisha are old college friends as well as my flatmates, so they will be my bridesmaids—the only ones.'

She paused. 'And, as, I'm going to be working abroad shortly, I couldn't be available for fittings with Ms FitzAlan, even if I wanted to.'

'On the contrary,' said Nigel Sylvester in a tone which made Maddie feel she'd been stranded naked on a polar ice cap. 'I think it is full time you recognised that you have responsibilities to my son that far outweigh your obligations to this—tin-pot job of yours, and hand your company a week's notice.'

Maddie lifted her chin. 'And you must also recognise I have no intention of abandoning my career.'

'Career?' he repeated almost meditatively. 'I think, my child, that you're deluding yourself.'

He then proceeded to deal quite mercilessly with her qualifications, her abilities and her ambitions, holding them up to ridicule, and dismissing them with quiet contempt, and all of it uttered with a smile like a naked blade held to her skin.

While all she could do was sit, head bent, in silence until it was over.

'How could you?' she flared at Jeremy when they were back in her own flat and alone, Sally and Trisha having taken a swift look at her white face and blazing eyes and tactfully disappeared to bed. 'I thought we'd already dealt with this. So how could you just sit there and let him speak to me—treat me like that?'

'I've told you time and again how he feels about working wives,' Jeremy said unhappily. 'And I've also tried to explain how Dad sees the importance of this wedding.'

She was about to hit back when she saw how wretched he was becoming and took a deep, steadying breath. It's not his fault, she reminded herself. His father has bullied him all his life. You know this.

'Darling,' she said. 'Esme and your father may have taken over most of the arrangements, but they're not adding me to their bag. I shall wear the dress I want, and have Sal and Trish as my backup on the day itself. No toddlers in sight. Not negotiable.'

He said slowly, 'But there's Italy. If I begged you not to go, would you think again?'

'I don't want you to beg,' she said more gently. 'Just to understand how much I want to research the Floria Bartrando story. I'll be gone a matter of days, that's all. It's not a problem.'

'It already is.' He shook his head. 'Dad's totally vitriolic on the subject, as if he's got a down on the entire Italian nation.'

'Your father simply has a down on not getting his own way at all times,' Maddie told him candidly. 'It wouldn't matter if it was Italy—or Outer Mongolia. However I can't and I won't give way to him, because that would set an unacceptable precedent. You must see that.'

She paused. 'Of course, we could always elope. Get a special licence and do the deed somewhere with a couple of strangers as witnesses.'

Jeremy looked at her with blank horror. 'You can't be serious.'

She hadn't been entirely joking either, she thought, suppressing a sigh.

She forced a smile. 'Alternatively, you could always come with me to Italy. Take a few days of all the leave you're owed and explore the delights of Liguria.' *And we could be alone as lovers again with no-one to interfere or disapprove. Get back to the time when we first fell in love. Wouldn't that be good?*

She added, 'And if I had you as an escort, that might placate your father about the trip in general.'

His mouth tightened. 'No,' he said. 'It wouldn't. And now I'd better go.' He took her in his arms and held her tightly. 'Oh, Maddie, I hate it when we quarrel.'

And I hate it when we have quarrels forced upon us, thought Maddie, fighting her disappointment as she kissed him and said goodnight.

And in the morning, she mused as she closed the door behind him, I shall have to tell the others it was a lovers' tiff. Pre-marital nerves or something. And see if they believe me.

Ironically, soon afterwards it began to seem as if Nigel Sylvester might get his own way after all.

Because Todd, her boss at Athene came within a whisker of calling the whole Bartrando project off.

'We need to know why a young singer with the world at her feet should simply disappear for thirty-odd years,' he'd said, frowning, at one of the morning conferences. 'We were promised a preliminary interview with Floria Bartrando herself, yet now they seem to be fobbing us off with a small provincial opera festival instead.' He snorted. 'And that's not worth the expense of the airfare, even if it is being sponsored by some local bigwig.'

'Perhaps she's making her comeback at this festival,' Maddie suggested, trying not to sound too anxious. If it all fell through, she could imagine Nigel Sylvester's triumph and the increased pressure to fall in with all future plans as a result.

Todd shrugged. 'Then, in that case, why don't they say so? I'm worried that this whole Bartrando thing could simply be a publicity stunt, and you'll end up being shown a grave in a cemetery and told that the festival's in her memory.'

'In which case, I use my return ticket, and we bin the entire project.' Maddie tried to sound upbeat. 'But I'm sure it's all going to work out.'

And a few days later when Todd summoned her to his office, it appeared she was right.

'I did the festival sponsor an injustice,' he announced, tapping the letter on the desk in front of him. 'He's written to us, in person, snail mail. His name's Count Valieri and he's apparently the link with Signorina Bartrando, so you'll be liaising with him.

'He'll have you met at the airport in Genoa and taken to the Hotel Puccini in Trimontano, where the festival will take place later in the year. And he'll contact you there and set up a meeting with the mystery lady.' He grinned. 'Maybe you should pack a posh frock if you're going to be hobnobbing with Italian aristocracy.'

'I'm more likely to be palmed off on some private secretary,' Maddie returned unruffled. 'But I'd better find out a bit about him, to be on the safe side.'

'I've already had a quick look online, and there isn't much.' Todd frowned. 'Just that the Valieri family actually started the festival over fifty years ago, so he's probably quite elderly, although there's no picture. And the family money now comes mainly from olive oil and ceramics. Apart from that—zilch.'

'Then it's fortunate we're not planning to tell his story.' She hesitated. 'Did he drop any hints about Signorina Bartrando?'

'Not one. Here, you'd better have it.' He handed her the sheet of elegant cream notepaper and she read the two short paragraphs.

The Count used black ink, she saw, and his handwriting was crisp and incisive.

Back in her office, she checked the hotel he'd

booked for her on the internet and saw it had an impressive number of stars, and its food and comfort were highly praised by recent guests.

So far, so good, she thought, wondering if Puccini's name was significant. After all, Floria Bartrando's first important role had been Musetta in 'La Boheme'. She'd received rave notices, completely eclipsing the woman playing Mimi. In fact, several critics thought she'd been miscast, and that her voice was more suited to the dramatic coloratura range of the leading part.

And her short but starry career had fully justified their opinion.

So maybe she simply disappeared because of death threats from other sopranos, thought Maddie, faintly amused.

But there'd been little to smile about since then. Jeremy had reacted badly to the news that her trip was definitely going ahead, and there'd been a definite coolness between them ever since. But that, she told herself, was probably due to his father giving him a hard time.

She had really hoped he would relent sufficiently to see her off at the airport, but there was no sign of him.

In the departure lounge she'd sent him a text— 'You'd better be pleased to see me when I get back', adding a row of kisses, but there'd been no response to that either and she'd boarded the plane, edgy and with the beginnings of a headache as she fought her disappointment.

When the trolley came round, she bought some orange juice and took a couple of painkillers, then settled back in her seat, deciding to close her eyes for a few moments.

But when the next sound she heard was the captain's voice announcing they had begun their descent to Cristoforo Columbo Airport, she realised, startled, just how tired she must have been.

As the plane turned inland, she caught her breath as she saw ahead of her, in fold after jagged fold, the peaks of the Apennines, some of them still streaked with snow.

She knew, of course, that in Italy, the mountains were never too far away, but these seemed almost too near. In some strange way—almost alien.

But she would begin an even closer acquaintance with them when she reached Trimontano, she reminded herself as the aircraft touched down.

While visualising them as threatening in some way was being over-imaginative, and showed the kind of stress she'd been under lately.

And which she'd come here to escape.

As she emerged from Arrivals, she was approached by a uniformed official.

'Signorina Lang?' His smile reassured her. 'I have been asked to escort you to the Count's car. Camillo, his driver, speaks no English.'

'Oh,' said Maddie. 'Well—that's very kind.'

This Count must be a real force to be reckoned with, she decided, as she was conducted through the terminal and out into the warm May sunlight to what appeared to be a private parking area, where a grizzled man in a chauffeur's uniform was waiting beside a limousine.

Well even if this turns out to be a journey to nowhere, Maddie thought with slight hysteria, as he inclined his head unsmilingly and opened the rear passenger door for her, at least I'll have travelled in style.

She'd been right, she told herself, leaning back against the cushions, to opt for a trim navy skirt rather than her usual jeans, although her jacket, which had received a faintly disparaging glance from Camillo, was denim. But she was glad of it once the car moved off, and the air conditioning came into play.

In front of her was a square leather case, which on investigation proved to be a cold box, containing bottled mineral water and fruit juice.

Every comfort, in fact, she thought. However, it would all have been rather more pleasant if Camillo had only spoken some English and she could have questioned him about their route and Trimontano itself.

He might even have been able to tell her something about Floria Bartrando's connection with this area, especially as the singer had been living and working far away in Rome just before her disappearance, and winning plaudits for her interpretation of Gilda in 'Rigoletto'.

But perhaps this should be left to the Count.

The port and its environs were soon left behind, the car powering its way through heavy traffic on a broad, busy road. Then, after about fifteen minutes, they turned on to another much narrower road, and, as if someone had flicked a switch, the landscape changed. No more urban sprawl or industrial development, but chestnut trees, olive groves and scrubby pastureland covering the foothills of the mountains, and the occasional scattered hamlet, clinging to the slopes.

The traffic they encountered now consisted mainly of farm wagons, groups of hikers sweating under large rucksacks, and packs of red-faced cyclists pounding up the increasingly steep ascent.

Maddie, drinking some water from the silver cup

provided for the purpose, was ignobly glad not to be of their number.

At the same time, she became aware that the brightness of the day had faded, and that heavy clouds were massing round the peaks in a frankly ominous way.

Bad weather would be disappointing, she thought with an inward shrug as the vision of sun-kissed villas and cypresses silhouetted against an azure sky began to fade, but, after all, she wasn't here as a holidaymaker.

Nor had she expected Trimontano to be quite so remote—not when it was the centre of an annual opera festival. The audiences would need to be serious music lovers to make this kind of journey.

And what had possessed Floria Bartrando to forsake the world stage and bury herself among these mountains?

There had to be a real story here if only she could unravel it, she thought, impatient to get to her destination and make a start.

A few minutes later, the car reached a fork in the road, and Camillo turned off to the right and began to descend into a valley, shadowed by a group of three tall peaks.

And there, suddenly, was Trimontano, like a toy town cupped in the hand of a stone giant.

Maddie leaned forward, eagerly scanning the clustering red roofs below her, noticing how a tall bell tower rose out of the midst of them, startlingly white and pointing towards the darkening sky like an accusing finger.

And at the same moment, like a warning voice reverberating between the mountains, came the first long, low rumble of thunder.

Heavens, thought Maddie, sinking back in her seat. That's a hell of an introduction. Good job I'm not superstitious, or I might just be having second thoughts.

It had already begun to rain when the car finally came to a stop in front of the massive portico of the Hotel Puccini in the main square.

A uniformed man, holding an umbrella, came down the steps to open the car door and shelter Maddie on her way into the hotel, while Camillo followed with her solitary bag.

Which should, of course, have been a matched set of Louis Vuitton, Maddie realised as she looked around at the expanse of marble, mirrors and gilded pillars which made up the hotel foyer. She turned to thank Camillo and found herself watching his retreating back.

He's clearly used to a better class of passenger,

she told herself ruefully as she walked to the reception desk.

But the receptionist's greeting passed no judgement, and the formalities were dealt with swiftly and efficiently.

'And there is also this, *signorina*.' He handed her an envelope along with her key card.

'From Count Valieri?' she asked.

'*Naturalmente*. On whose behalf, I am to welcome you to Trimontano.' He smiled, making a slight bow. 'You are in Number 205, *signorina*. The lift is behind you, and your luggage is already in your room. If you need further assistance you have only to ask.'

Rule one in a strange town—know the right people, Maddie thought as the lift took her smoothly to her floor.

Her bedroom was more modern than she had imagined, with an impressive range of fitted furniture in an elegant pale wood, together with the widest bed she had ever seen.

The bathroom was breathtaking too, tiled in white marble, streaked with gold. It had a large sunken tub with two cushioned head-rests, and a walk-in shower also big enough for dual occupation, and then some.

The ultimate in togetherness, Maddie thought,

suppressing a pang of regret that she was there alone. But even if Jeremy was far away, at least she could talk to him.

She went back in the bedroom and retrieved her mobile phone from her bag, only to discover to her dismay that there was no discernible signal.

'Let's hope that's because of the prevailing weather conditions and not a general rule,' she muttered, as she dialled reception from the bed-side phone and asked for an outside line.

But she had another disappointment when, after a struggle to get through, Jeremy's voicemail informed her he was out of the office.

Sighing, she replaced the receiver without leaving a message. After all, she'd nothing to tell him about her trip that he'd want to hear. The important thing had been to hear his voice, even if it was only a recording. Crumbs from the rich man's table, she thought ironically. Speaking of which…

She reached for the Count's envelope and tore it open.

'And if this is to say that Floria Bartrando won't see me, then I'll know bad luck really does run in threes,' she said as she unfolded the single sheet of paper it contained. As she did so, another smaller, flimsier strip of paper fluttered to the carpet.

Maddie picked it up and found she was looking

at a ticket for the opera that night at the Teatro Grande. 'Verdi's 'Rigoletto,' she whispered to herself in excitement. 'Floria's last appearance. This has to be significant.'

The accompanying note, written in the familiar black ink said only 'Until later', and was signed 'Valieri'.

A man of few words, the Count, thought Maddie joyfully. But what does that matter, bless every grey hair on his probably balding head?

And she kissed the ticket and laughed out loud, because it had proved to be third time lucky instead and she was in business.

CHAPTER THREE

AS THE CURTAIN fell on Act Two, Maddie sank back in her seat with a breathless sigh. She had forgotten how dark the plot of 'Rigoletto' was with its curses, vendettas, seductions and betrayal, and the hunchback jester seeking vengeance on his lecherous master. But she'd certainly never forgotten Verdi's glorious music.

And the beautiful aria *'Caro nome'* where the doomed Gilda rhapsodises about her lover's name was still singing in her head as the lights came up. It had featured on one of Floria Bartrando's few albums, and Maddie had acquired a second-hand CD, playing it constantly while she was preparing for her trip, and bringing it with her.

The Teatro Grande wasn't quite as large as its name suggested, but its Baroque styling was magnificent, she thought, glancing up at the semi-circle of ornately decorated boxes above her.

During the first act interval, she had been convinced that someone up there was watching her, and had looked up, scanning the boxes eagerly in the hope of catching a glimpse of the Count, or even Floria Bartrando herself.

If she had been the subject of scrutiny, she hoped she'd passed muster. Wisely, she'd brought her favourite and most expensive dress, a simple black knee-length shift, square-necked and sleeveless, relying totally on cut and its heavy silk fabric for its stunning effect.

She'd left her hair loose but swept back from her face with silver combs, and apart from the silver studs in her ears, her only jewellery was Jeremy's diamond solitaire on her engagement finger.

She followed the rest of the audience to the small crowded bar and took her double espresso to a small table with a single chair in a quiet corner. As she sat, she noticed the picture on the wall above her. It was a large oil painting in a heavy gilded frame, its subject a seated man, white-haired but still handsome with a calm, proud face. A small plaque read 'Cesare Valieri'.

So this is my host, she thought. And where is he?

She leaned across to the attendant, clearing a nearby table. 'Count Valieri—is he here tonight?'

He hesitated, his glance sliding away. 'He came, *signorina*, for a brief time, but has gone. I am sorry.'

Well, it didn't really matter, she told herself, suppressing a pang of disappointment. They would meet eventually. And at least now she knew what to expect.

And her instinct about being watched might well have been correct, so it seemed odd that he had not used the opportunity to make himself known to her.

She settled back in her seat for Act III, waiting for the tragedy to reach its culmination, with Gilda sacrificing herself to save the villainous Duke who had seduced and betrayed her.

Shivering as Rigoletto tells his hired assassin 'He is crime and I am punishment.'

And feeling tears prick at her eyelids as the jester realising he has brought about the murder of his own child, flings himself, heartbroken, across her dead body.

The applause at the end was long and generous with cries of '*Bravo*' from all over the auditorium. It took a while for the stalls to clear and Maddie hung back, unsure what she should do.

Her best bet, she supposed, was to go back to the hotel and wait for instructions. Because she was sure there would be some.

In a way, she hoped they'd arrive tomorrow. It was late, and she felt suddenly very tired, as she walked out into the rain-washed street, hugging her cream pashmina around her. The stress of the past weeks coupled with the flight and the long car journey were clearly taking their toll.

I need sleep, she thought longingly, not an interview.

But the Count clearly had other ideas, she realised, recognising the unmistakable shape of his limousine, parked just across the street from the theatre, with its chauffeur in his dark uniform standing beside it holding the rear passenger door open for her.

And not Camillo this time. This new man was altogether taller and leaner. Younger too, she thought, although his peaked cap was pulled down shadowing his face, denying her a good look.

'Signorina Lang—you will come with me, please.' His voice was quiet, but it seemed to convey an order rather than a request, and Maddie hesitated.

'You're taking me to the Count?'

'Who does not like to be kept waiting.'

Slightly brusque for a paid employee, she thought as she climbed into the car, but at least he spoke English, so that was a step forward.

Not that any conversation was likely, however,

while the glass panels between the front and rear seating remained firmly closed.

On the other hand, she didn't really feel like talking. The effect of the coffee had worn off and waves of drowsiness were sweeping over her.

But I can't go to sleep, she told herself firmly, suppressing a yawn. I have to stay awake and totally alert. This is an important evening. And made herself check once again that her little voice operated tape machine and spare batteries were safely in her bag.

What she really needed was the caffeine rush from another espresso, she thought, helping herself to some of the chilled mineral water, in the hope that it would clear her head.

She began to rehearse some of the questions she needed to ask, but instead found the words and music of the opera still teeming through her brain.

I am Crime. He is Punishment. Except that was wrong, surely. It was the other way round. *He is Crime...*

Wasn't that the way it went? She wasn't even sure any more. But she could remember Rigoletto's despairing cry, 'Ah, the curse' and shivered again.

She wanted to knock on the glass and ask the chauffeur not to drive quite so fast, but it was too much effort. Somehow it was much easier just to lean back against the cushions, and let them support her until the jolting over the cobbled streets ceased.

I'll close my eyes for a few minutes, she told herself, yawning again. A little catnap. I'll feel better then. Wide awake. Ready for anything.

And let herself slide gently down into a soft, welcoming cloud of darkness.

Her first conscious thought was that the car had stopped moving at last, and she no longer felt as if she was being shaken to bits.

Her next—that she was no longer simply sitting down, but lying flat as if she was on a couch. Or even a bed.

With a supreme effort, she lifted her heavy lids and discovered that she was indeed in a bed.

Oh God, I must have been taken ill, she thought, forcing herself to sit up. And I'm back at the hotel.

But just one glance round the room disabused her of that notion.

For one thing, the bed she was lying in, though just as wide and comfortable as the one in Room 205, was clearly very much older with an elegant headboard in some dark wood, and a sumptuous crimson brocade coverlet.

For another, there seemed to be doors everywhere, she realised in bewilderment as she tried desperately to focus. Doors next to each other, in some impossible way, in every wall all round the large square room. Doors painted in shades of green, blue and pink, and interspersed with shuttered windows.

I'm not awake, she thought, falling limply back against the pillows. I can't be because this is obviously some weird dream.

She wasn't even wearing her own white lawn nightdress, but some astonishing garment in heavy sapphire silk with narrow straps and a deeply plunging neckline. And it was the faint shiver of the expensive fabric against her skin that finally convinced her that she wasn't dreaming. And that she hadn't fallen down a rabbit hole like Alice either.

The bed and this extraordinary door-filled room were not Wonderland at all, but total, if puzzling, reality.

Go back to your first conclusion, she told herself. You became ill in the Count's car, and you were brought here to recover. That's the only feasible explanation, even if you don't remember feeling unwell—just terribly sleepy.

And you've been looked after, although a room

liable to give one hallucinations was perhaps not the best choice in the circumstances.

Thinking back, she seemed to remember a phrase which described this kind of décor. *Trompe l'oeil*, she thought. That was it. She'd come across it during some of her preliminary research on the Ligurian region, but had decided it was irrelevant.

However, it occurred to her that she was growing a little tired of mysteries and enigmas, whether verbal or visual, and would relish a little straight talking from here on in.

She would also prefer to get dressed, she thought, if only she knew where her clothes were.

She wondered too what time it was—and that was when she realised, with shock, that not only was she no longer wearing her wristwatch, but that, even more alarmingly, her engagement ring was also missing.

And it's not just my clothes, she thought frantically, as she shot bolt upright, suddenly wide awake as she stared round the room. Where's my bag? My money, passport, credit cards, mobile phone, tape recorder—everything?

Suddenly, the fact that she was next door to naked in a strange bed, in a strange house in the middle of God only knew where, took on a new and frightening significance.

And even if there was a perfectly innocent explanation, the noble Count Valieri was going to have some serious explaining to do—when they finally met.

The next moment, Maddie heard a key rattle, and a section of the wall opposite the bed swung open, revealing that, in this case, it was a real door and not a pretence.

But it was not the man in the portrait, her expected elderly host who entered. Her visitor was male but younger, tall, lean, olive-skinned and, in some strange way, familiar. Yet how could that be? she asked herself, perplexed, when she was quite certain that she'd never seen that starkly chiselled, arrogant face before in her life, or those amazing golden brown eyes, currently flicking over her with something very near disdain.

'So you have woken at last.'

It was the voice that jogged her memory. The cool, peremptory tones she'd last heard ordering her into the Count's car outside the opera house. Only now, instead of the chauffeur's tunic and peaked cap of their previous encounter, he was wearing chinos and a black polo shirt, unbuttoned at his tanned throat, this casual dress emphasising the width of his shoulders, the narrowness of his hips and his long legs. He looked strong and tough without an ounce of excess weight.

A factor that only served to increase her unease, which she knew she must be careful not to show.

However, realising how much of her the sapphire nightgown was revealing in turn, she made a belated snatch at the embroidered linen sheet.

'Obviously,' she returned with a snap, angrily aware of a faintly derisive smile curling his hard mouth. She paused, taking a deep, calming breath. 'You're the Count's driver, so presumably you brought me here.' *Wherever here is.*

'*Sì, signorina.*'

'The problem is I can't quite remember what happened. Have I been ill? And how long have I been asleep?'

He shrugged. 'About twelve hours.'

'Twelve hours?' Maddie repeated. Then, her voice rising, 'That long?

That's impossible.'

'You fell asleep in the car. And you were still *morta*—sleeping like the dead when we arrived.'

'Then how did I get here—like this?'

'I carried you,' he said. Adding, 'And you continued to sleep quite happily in my arms as I did so.'

Her mouth went dry as she assimilated that. 'I don't believe you,' she said hoarsely. 'There must have been something—in the coffee. Or that water in the car. You drugged me.'

His mouth tightened. 'Now you are being absurd,' he stated coldly.

She waved an impatient hand. 'Well—maybe. But I don't understand why you didn't take me back to my hotel.'

'Because the Count wished you to be brought here.'

'Well, that was kind of him—I suppose. But I prefer to stick to my own arrangements. Perhaps you would thank him and tell him I'd like to leave.'

'That will not be possible. You are going nowhere, *signorina*. You will remain here until arrangements for your release have been concluded with your family in Britain.'

There was a taut silence, then Maddie said unevenly, 'Are you telling me that I've been kidnapped?'

'Yes,' he said, adding laconically, 'I regret the necessity.'

'Oh you're going to have regrets all right,' she said, her voice shaking. 'When you find yourself in court. And don't think a plea of insanity will spare you.'

'I would not think of offering one, even if there were to be a court case—which I guarantee there will not.' He paused. 'And I am completely rational, I assure you.'

'In which case,' Maddie said stormily, 'you can prove it by returning my belongings and arranging for that other man—Camillo—to take me to Trimontano for the rest. Instantly.'

'That is not going to happen. Your possessions have already been collected from the hotel and brought here.'

Maddie gasped. 'Who decided this?'

'I did.'

'Then here's a decision that I've made,' she said icily. 'I came to Italy to interview a woman who was once a singer called Floria Bartrando. I don't suppose you've heard of her.'

'The name is familiar.'

'You amaze me.' She gave him a stony look. 'Your boss, Count Valieri was supposed to be acting as go-between, and I understood there was a need for a measure of secrecy about the project. But this—abduction—this is total madness. And it stops here.

'The deal over the Bartrando interview is off, and I'm leaving as soon as I get my luggage back.'

'And I say that you stay as you are and where you are.' He added softly, 'Until I choose otherwise.'

He walked towards the bed, and, in spite of her

previous resolution, Maddie found herself shrinking back against the pillows. She said, 'Don't come near me. Don't dare to touch me.'

He halted, his mouth twisting contemptuously. 'You flatter yourself, *signorina*. Let me assure you that your body is of no interest to me, except as a commodity to be exchanged when my negotiations with your family are complete.'

She was silent, thoughts scurrying through her head. She knew of course that people were taken hostage, but these were mainly wealthy tourists who'd strayed into dangerous places. Not a TV researcher looking for a lost soprano in a supposedly civilised backwater.

She said slowly, 'You—you really mean you're holding me for ransom? That I'm your hostage?'

He frowned. 'A crude term. Let us say instead that you will remain here as my guest until the deal is done.'

'Then I'll be here for a bloody long time,' she flung back at him. 'My God, now I know you're crazy. My family haven't that sort of money. My uncle's the headmaster of a school, and my aunt helps in a local nursery. So they couldn't pay you in a hundred years.'

'But I was not talking about them. I was referring to the family you are about to marry into—

who are rich,' he said quietly, sending a chill down her spine. 'And it will cost them a great deal to get you back—unharmed.'

Maddie stared up at the dark, cold face, her lips parted in shock.

She thought, 'He wants money from Jeremy and his father? But why? Just because they're wealthy?'

She said, her voice shaking, 'You can't possibly mean this.'

'Have I not made it clear that I do?'

'But you can't have thought about the consequences,' she persisted. 'You'll get years in jail when you're caught. Your life will be wasted.'

She saw his mouth harden, and his eyes fill with unutterable bleakness. He looked, she thought, as if he too had been carved from limestone like the nearby mountains.

He said, 'Then I would not be the first. But you argue in vain, *signorina,* because no charges against me will ever be brought.'

'But what about the Count? He's a respected man. A businessman. A patron of the arts.' She spoke almost wildly, clutching at straws. 'You can't tell me he knows what you're doing.'

'You are wrong. He knows everything.'

'And condones it?' Maddie shook her head. 'No, I don't—I won't believe it.'

'Then ask him,' he said. 'At dinner this evening. I am here to invite you to join him.'

'Then you can both go to hell.' She glared at him. 'Do you really imagine I'd sit down to a meal with someone who treats me like this? I'd rather starve.'

'Do so, then.' His tone was indifferent. 'If your future husband responds swiftly to my demands, you should not have to endure many days of hunger.'

'You mean—you wouldn't care?'

'That you wish to behave like a fool? That is your choice. But I think you would do better to accept the situation, so that you look like a woman and not a skeleton on your wedding day.'

He paused. 'There is a bell beside the bed. Ring it and a maid will come, and bring anything you require.'

'All I want,' Maddie told him tersely, 'is a way out of here.'

'That, I fear, she cannot provide. And she is loyal to the Count, like the rest of his staff,' he added. 'So do not ask.'

She said shortly, 'I'm hardly in a position to bribe anyone.' She hesitated. 'Nor am I exactly dressed for dinner—even with a geriatric kidnapper. Will I get my clothes back?'

'You will be provided with adequate covering,' he said. 'Be content with that.'

Which was another way of saying 'no', Maddie thought as he walked back across the room and the door—a blue one—closed behind him, becoming just part of the wall again.

She lay staring at it while she counted to fifty slowly, to make quite sure that he'd gone, before she pushed away the coverlet and swung out of bed, treading across the marble floor to try the handle. But the door was locked, as she'd known in her heart that it would be.

However, that could not be the only real door in the room. And now she would find the others.

The first she came across gave access to a large walk in closet, lined on one side with drawers in the same dark wood as the bed-head, all empty, with a matching series of wardrobes filling the opposite wall.

Maddie pulled open each door in turn, but the interior rail held nothing but a robe that matched the nightgown she was wearing, and a pair of velvet slippers in the same deep blue.

'His idea of adequate covering, no doubt,' she muttered as she closed the door again and went back into the bedroom.

What she really needed to find was the bathroom, but naturally she wouldn't have lowered herself by asking him where it was. And her dogged search revealed it behind a pink door a couple of doors away from the closet.

The dark green marble walls, she thought, made it gloomy, although that might have reflected her own mood, rather than the décor, while the bathtub and shower were both distinctly old-fashioned.

However, the water was hot and the plumbing worked. There were plenty of towels and a basic selection of toiletries, none of them her own.

There was also a full length mirror on one of the walls and she stood for a moment staring at her reflection.

Your body is of no interest to me...

Out of all the things he'd said to her, why on earth should she remember those words in particular? Impossible, she thought, to fathom.

At the same time she could not help noticing, albeit unwillingly, how the deep bodice of the nightgown gently cupped her breasts and the way the cling of the fabric swirled as she moved, the silk hem just brushing her insteps.

No interest. Yet the right size, she thought, and the right length. And although the colour and style of the nightgown were not something she would ever have chosen for herself, she could not deny that it was becoming, making her fair hair look almost silvery.

What was more, she would swear it was brand new, and she wondered, as she turned away, who it had been bought for originally.

But, she reminded herself briskly, she had far more pressing matters to consider. Her priority was to get out of this crazy, dangerous situation and somehow reach Genoa, the airport and safety.

She knew now which were the real doors and which the false, and accepted that there was no opportunity for escape there. So, she started on the windows. The first two sets of shutters opened on to glorious oil-painted landscapes—one showing a sylvan lake overlooked by a rococo palace—the other depicting rolling meadows studded with poppies and edged by cypress trees.

The Italy I was expecting to find, she thought wryly, walking on to the next window, and catching her breath as she flung back the shutters.

Because there were the mountains as far as her eyes could see, confronting her, surrounding her like a cage of rock. And, in spite of the sunshine, as tall, harsh and inimical as her jailer, she thought, feeling suddenly cold.

While one gingerly downwards glance told her

that below the window was a sheer drop to heaven knows where.

And there was no sign of Trimontano, or any other human habitation apart from the prison she was standing in.

She left the shutters open, and went back to lie on the bed, heaping the pillows up behind her as she began a serious attempt to evaluate her equally serious position.

Her only hope seemed to lie with Count Valieri himself, who surely could not know that an actual crime was being perpetrated in his name. Not unless the younger man had some hold on him too and was forcing him into it.

If this was the case, then maybe they could work together to stop things before they went too far. Unless of course the Count was older and feebler than his portrait at the theatre suggested.

But that couldn't be true. His handwriting suggested a forceful and determined personality, so he might well be acting against his better judgement for some reason.

So, she would simply have to talk him round, she thought. Tell him frankly that Nigel Sylvester was also a forceful and determined man, and certainly not someone you would wish to have as an enemy, and to treat him as prey would undoubtedly have a dangerous backlash.

She could also warn the Count that she wasn't Nigel Sylvester's favourite person and, if it was left to him, he probably wouldn't give a brass farthing to get her back.

Perhaps not in those exact words, she thought ruefully. But at least I can let him know that if this madness continues, he'll have a fight on his hands that he can't possibly win.

While I, she thought, her throat tightening nervously. I could end up caught helplessly in the middle. And what will happen to me then?

CHAPTER FOUR

SHE SEEMED TO have lost all track of time. But maybe that was a deliberate policy of disorientation on the part of her captors.

Eventually, of course, she had rung the bell, unable to ignore her stomach's wistful rumblings any longer, and recognising, too, that she needed to keep her strength up.

A maid had appeared so promptly she might have been waiting outside the door, and carrying a small table which she placed beside the bed. She was followed by another girl in a starched white overall, her hair covered by a cap, and carrying a laden tray. After which they nodded, smiled, wished her '*Buon appetito*' and left.

And this time, she actually heard the key turn in the lock.

And they'd behaved as if it was perfectly normal to serve a strange girl locked in a bedroom, wearing nothing but a nightdress in the middle of the day. A realisation which did nothing to lift her spirits.

Sighing, Maddie investigated the tray and found a tureen of vegetable soup, steaming and aromatic with herbs, a linen napkin containing freshly baked rolls, a plate of cold meats, and, in a covered glass dish, a scarily rich dessert that seemed to be composed from chocolate truffles. There was also a small jug of red wine, a bottle of mineral water and a pot of excellent black coffee.

It would have been more dignified to pick at the food, but Maddie fell on it as if she hadn't eaten for a week.

Last night's dinner was a long time ago, she told herself as she wiped out the few final delicious drops from her soup bowl with a crust, and tonight's confrontation was unlikely to be relaxed or festive. So she'd make the most of what there was, although she was sparing with the wine, knowing that later she would need to keep her wits about her.

But it took a very long afternoon to get to that point. When the maid returned for the tray, she brought with her a lamp with a pretty glass shade which she placed on the table. But when Maddie asked if she could have a book to read, the girl murmured an apologetic *'Non capisco,'* and left.

So there was nothing to do except allow the same weary thoughts turn like a treadmill in her brain, and watch the afternoon light begin to fade from the sky.

She even took a bath, just to break the monotony, but the warm water failed to have its usual soothing effect.

It was disturbing to consider how carefully her capture must have been planned and executed. And know it was her connection with the Sylvesters that had condemned her to this nerve-racking experience.

But I shall be blamed for it, she told herself. Because I insisted on coming to Italy.

Suddenly she had lost control of her life, she realised as trailed back into the bedroom, swathed in a towel. And the knowledge made her feel vulnerable. And scared.

Although the Count's henchman had said she would be returned 'unharmed'. And that was the word she had to cling to, hoping against hope that her captors meant it.

But all those trick doors were a reminder of how completely she was trapped. And if she was going to be left to vegetate all day and every day, she'd be stark raving mad by the time the ransom was paid. If indeed that ever happened...

The next time the real door opened, it was already quite dark and she'd lit the lamp. She sat up nervously, wishing she was wearing more than a towel, but it wasn't her kidnapper but another maid, a short stocky girl, who'd brought with her Maddie's own hairbrush and cosmetics bag.

But nothing else.

The girl gave her an unsmiling nod as she walked into the bathroom, emerging a moment later, her face set in lines of disapproval as she shook non-existent creases from the nightgown Maddie had left on the floor after her bath. She placed it carefully on the bed, then fetched the matching robe which she laid beside it.

She said, 'You dress please, *signorina*.' Her English was halting and heavily accented, but at least it was communication, thought Maddie, wishing it had been the girl who smiled.

'Willingly,' she returned. 'When I get my clothes back.'

The girl pointed at the gleaming blue silk on the bed. 'This—clothes for you. Is time to eat, so please hurry.'

'Of course, the Count doesn't like to be kept waiting. I almost forgot.' Maddie's tone was sarcastic. 'Perhaps it would cause less inconvenience if I left him to dine alone.'

'*E impossibile.*' The other spoke firmly. 'He asks for you. Not good to make angry, *signorina.*'

'You mean he might send his enforcer to fetch me?' Maddie saw the girl's bewildered look and shook her head. 'Oh, it doesn't matter.'

Besides, she needed to talk him round not provoke his anger, she reminded herself as she went into the bathroom to change. So she would do as she was told—at first, anyway.

Once it was on, she discovered that the robe was cut on severe lines with high lapels and a full skirt, which revealed very little. Once Maddie had wound its long sash twice round her slender waist and fastened it with a secure bow, she felt rather better about her unorthodox appearance. She used no make-up, and simply brushed her hair loose on her shoulders.

She looked pale, she thought, wrinkling her nose, as she turned away from the mirror. But it would be impolitic to go in with all guns blazing, and besides, with a subdued approach, the Count might see her as a victim and take pity on her.

'Some chance,' she muttered under her breath as she returned to the bedroom, where the maid was waiting with ill-concealed impatience.

'*Fa presto, signorina,*' she said, leading the way to the door.

Following, Maddie saw a bunch of keys attached to the girl's belt, half hidden by her apron. She considered the chances of snatching them and running, and decided they were poor. Even if she took the girl by surprise, her adversary's sturdy build would make her difficult to overpower, while the other side of the door was unknown territory.

Be patient and bide your time, she told herself. It will come.

At the door she paused. 'What is your name?' she asked.

'Domenica, *signorina*.' The reply was brusque. '*Andiamo*.'

Maddie walked out into a long passage, dimly lit, with a short flight of steps at its end, and a curtained archway at their foot.

Domenica set a brisk pace, and Maddie, in her trailing skirts, struggled to keep up with her. At the end, the girl waited, tight-lipped, holding back the curtain for Maddie to pass in front of her.

She stepped out on to a wide galleried landing, and found herself looking down at a room as large as a medieval hall, panelled in wood, and reached by a broad, curving staircase.

In the centre was a vast refectory table, surrounded by high-backed chairs, while a pair of dark brown leather sofas flanked a stone fireplace where logs were burning.

One of the few cheerful signs she'd encountered so far, she thought. As was the imposing bird cage hanging from a bracket in one of the corners.

And at the far end of the room was a grand piano, indicating the Count was not just an opera patron, but musical himself.

But, at the moment, the room was clearly unoccupied and she hesitated, glancing at Domenica who pointed expressionlessly at the stairs, then turned and disappeared back the way she'd come.

Like someone else on the Count's staff, her people skills could use some work, thought Maddie, lifting her skirts slightly in order to descend the stone treads in safety.

And if her host was such a stickler for punctuality, why wasn't he waiting there to offer an explanation for this outrage? To be followed by profuse apologies and offers of generous redress for the fright and inconvenience she'd suffered.

Nothing less would do, as she would make clear when he eventually showed up, she thought, noting thankfully that only two places had been set at the table.

And while she was waiting, she could take another and more thorough look round this amazing room.

But it didn't take long to realise that her eye had been tricked all over again because there wasn't a genuine inch of panelling anywhere, only skillfully applied paint. Even the splendid birdcage with its resident macaw was a clever three-dimensional deception.

And of the pair of imposing double doors flanking the staircase, only one would ever open—or it might when unlocked, Maddie acknowledged, vainly twisting the wrought iron handle.

But at least the fire was a living thing, she thought, and it might help to dispel the inevitable chill of tension. As she walked across the room, her attention was caught by the massive painting hanging over the mantelpiece.

An initial glance suggested that it was one of the Count's favourite dogs—a German Shepherd immortalised in oils as it stood, king-like, on a high, flat rock against a grey and stormy sky. But then she realised that the shape of the head, the length of the snout, the colouring were all wrong. That this creature was far from being anyone's loved domestic pet. Nor would it ever be used to guard sheep, or not by a shepherd with a brain.

My God, she thought incredulously, staring upwards. It's a wolf.

And didn't realise she'd spoken aloud until a voice she recognised said softly, '*Sì, signorina*—you are quite right. Allow me to bid you a belated welcome to Casa Lupo. To—the House of the Wolf.'

Maddie swung round with a gasp, aware that her heart seemed to be beating a warning tattoo against her ribcage.

He was standing a few yards away, as a whole section of the false panelling closed noiselessly behind him.

He was slightly more formally clad than earlier, but that was little comfort when his elegant black pants fitted him like a second skin, and his white silk shirt was unbuttoned sufficiently to display several inches of bronzed chest. In fact, in some inexplicable way, it served to make him look even more formidable.

Maddie had to make a conscious effort not to take a step backwards.

'What are you doing here?' she demanded.

The dark brows lifted. 'I intend to have dinner. What else?'

She lifted her chin. 'Does the Count usually dine with his staff?' she asked coldly.

'If he wishes,' he said, unfazed. 'Why not?'

'Isn't it perfectly obvious?' She glared at him. 'Because I hoped—I really hoped I wouldn't have to see you again.'

His slight shrug conveyed indifference. 'Then let us both hope this is the worst disappointment you have to suffer,' he retorted.

'But the Count will be joining us surely?' She could not hide her dismay.

'Perhaps later, if he so chooses. Is it important?'

'Of course it is.' Her voice was husky. 'I need to talk to him—to persuade him to see reason.'

'A waste of breath. Your views will not affect his plans in any way.'

'So you say.' Maddie's tone was ragged. 'How do I know he isn't just another of your victims, banged up for ransom somewhere.'

'Your imagination is running away with you. The Count Valieri is a free agent conducting his own affairs. Therefore I suggest you relax and trust that your *fidanzato*'s family act quickly to effect your release.'

'And if they don't?'

He shrugged again. 'Then, unhappily, pressure will be brought to bear.' His deliberate pause allowed her to consider the implications of that. 'But let us hope for the best.'

There was a rattle of the door at the back of the room, and the smiling maid came in wheeling a trolley laden with bottle and glasses.

'So why not relax,' he continued. 'And join me in an *aperitivo*.'

'Thank you, but no.' Maddie gave him a scornful look. 'This is hardly a social occasion.'

'I believe you enjoy white wine with soda,' he went on as if she hadn't spoken.

And exactly how had he come by that scrap of personal information? Maddie wondered with a sudden thud of the heart.

Aloud, she said, 'It's not just your alcohol that I find unacceptable, but your company. Strangely, I've no wish to spend any more time with the Count's hired thug. I'd have thought he could have spared me that.'

'He tends to leave such decisions to me.'

'His mistake.' Maddie glanced towards the stairs. 'But it need not be mine. So, I'd like to go back to my solitary confinement. Right now.'

'You will remain here,' he said. 'In fact, I insist upon it.'

He turned to the maid and gave her a softly voiced instruction in their own language.

Almost within seconds a perfectly made spritzer was placed in Maddie's reluctant hand.

Childishly, she wanted to throw it over him. To watch it drip from his hair and soak his shirt, and see that cool impassivity splinter into something relatively human.

Except that provoking him into any kind of humanity might not be the wisest choice she'd ever made.

Instead, she gritted her teeth and said, '*Grazie.*'

'*Prego.*' The girl beamed as she poured a measure of Scotch into an elegant crystal tumbler and handed it to Maddie's companion, before whisking herself away through the door at the back of the room.

Leaving them alone again.

There was an odd silence, then he raised his glass. '*Salute.*'

Maddie paused, then responded with such open reluctance that the hard mouth slanted into a grin.

'Let me guess,' he said. 'Instead of drinking to my health, you would prefer to see me dead at your feet.'

She shrugged. 'Why should I pretend?' She paused. 'You speak very good English. Acquired by preying on tourists, I suppose.'

His grin widened wickedly. 'If they permit me to do so—why not?'

She felt an odd, unwelcome tingle of sensation feather down her spine.

She hurried into speech. 'May I ask you something?'

'Perhaps. Unless it is another request to see the Count. I am beginning to find your persistence in this matter a bore.'

'Well, we can't have that, can we?' Maddie said, poisonously sweet. 'The Count mustn't be kept waiting. You mustn't be bored. I'll try to remember.'

'It would be a favour.' He paused. 'What do you wish to know?'

'I would like to know where all my possessions have gone.' She gestured almost helplessly. 'Particularly my engagement ring and my watch. They could surely be returned. I—I miss them.'

'And you must continue to do so, I fear. Along with certain documents, they are on their way to London as additional proof that you are in our charge.'

'How can you do this?' Her voice shook. 'Jeremy will be devastated—out of his mind with shock and worry.'

'A further incentive for the Sylvesters to come quickly to terms,' he retorted. 'If they do so, your diamond should be glittering safely on your hand again very soon.

'As for your watch,' he added, his tone faintly caustic. 'You will find the hours pass in much the same way without you keeping track of them. They may even go faster.'

'But you surely can't have sent my clothes to London as well, and I want them. I need them.' She gestured at herself. 'You can't expect me to wear these things all day and every day. It—it's degrading.'

'Degrading?' he repeated. 'I do not think you know the meaning of the word. However your own clothing will be returned when I feel you will no longer be tempted to escape and not before.

'Besides what you are wearing covers you from your throat to your ankles,' he added, the amber gaze sweeping her. 'Quite unlike the dress you wore to the opera yesterday evening, if I am permitted to say so.'

'Yes, she said. 'My dress and—other things.' She took a deep breath. 'You carried me to my room, but I'd like to know—who undressed me?'

'I am tempted to pretend,' he said silkily. 'But I shall not do so. It was Domenica.'

She bit her lip. 'I suppose I must be grateful for that at least.'

'And for much else, let us hope. You will find that the Count employs an excellent cook.'

Restive under his gaze, Maddie moved away down the room, stopping to look up at the painted cage and its silent inmate. 'Why is nothing as it seems in this house?'

'It is a style of decoration much favoured in this part of the world. You will become accustomed to it.'

'I trust I'll be away from here long before that can happen.' She took a sip of her drink and wandered over to the baby grand. 'At least this is real.' She played a note and paused. 'Is the Count a pianist?'

He shrugged. 'He had lessons in childhood, but he would tell you that he is no virtuoso, and plays for his own amusement. Why do you ask?'

She swung round, staring at him defiantly. 'Because it baffles me how a man with any claim to culture could behave in this barbaric way.'

'That might depend on how you define barbarism,' he said softly. 'You may have heard it said that the end justifies the means.'

'Oh, really?' she asked scornfully. 'And what possible justification can there be for abducting a total stranger?'

'You are far from that. A great deal about you

is known. Your age, your work, your relationships, your size in clothing. Even your preference in drinks.'

He added, 'And it is a question of reparation. You are simply unfortunate in being the instrument by which this can be achieved.'

'And that gives you the right to keep me as a prisoner?' Maddie's tone bit. 'I don't think so.'

'You are merely being caused some minor inconvenience, *signorina*.' His voice was equally curt. 'You would find genuine captivity far worse, believe me.'

'Something you and your boss will experience at first hand very soon, I hope.' She drew a jerky breath. 'You'll find to your cost that Mr Sylvester is a very unforgiving man.'

'But so is Count Valieri. Which is something he has had to wait a long time to prove.' He paused, then added quietly, 'Maddalena.'

The breath seemed to catch suddenly in her throat. 'That,' she said huskily, 'is not my name.'

'Not in your language perhaps, but in mine.'

'Well, I did not give you permission to use either version.'

'*Che peccato.*' He drank some whisky, watching her reflectively over the top of the glass. 'Whereas you, *naturalmente*, are entirely free to call me Andrea, if you wish.'

She lifted her chin defiantly. 'And here's another well-known saying for you, *signore*.' She laid stress on each individual word. 'In—your—dreams.'

That grin was playing about his lips again. 'I think my dreams are already stimulating enough,' he drawled. 'But I will bear your suggestion in mind.' He paused. 'And now, perhaps, you will join me at the table. Our dinner is being served.'

In some other dimension, she might have sat stony-faced, refusing everything put in front of her. In the real world, to her shame, she ate everything put in front of her from the dishes of *antipasti*, to the fillets of fish in their creamy sauce accompanied by asparagus spears, and the delectable veal casserole, fragrant with wine and tiny spring vegetables.

Finally, there was cheese, and rich *pannacotta* served with a thick red berry sauce.

And, of course, wine. A crisp Orvieto to begin with, and a full-bodied Montepulciano to follow. While, with the coffee came *grappa,* innocently colourless yet heart-stoppingly potent in the tiny glasses as Maddie discovered with her first cautious sip.

And all this regardless of the sardonic gaze of the man lounging in the high-backed chair at the head of the table.

It occurred to her reluctantly that she could not fault her captor in his role as stand-in host. No matter how monosyllabic her replies, he continued to chat as if this was a normal dinner party and she the guest of honour.

Good manners, she asked herself wryly, or just unmitigated gall?

The opera was one of the topics touched on.

'You enjoyed it?'

'It's a dark, grim story,' she returned. 'Perhaps it should have been a warning to me.'

He laughed. 'You think you will be disposed of and stuffed into a sack like Gilda?' He shook his head. 'What a tragic waste that would be.'

'Am I supposed to find that reassuring?'

He shrugged. 'It is the truth. Make of it what you will.'

She played with the stem of her glass. 'When does the Count expect a message back from London?'

'He has received one already, but merely to say that the papers and the evidence that you are his guest have been safely delivered at their destination. Now the matter rests with your *fidanzato* and his father.'

She gasped. 'Then I could be out of here in forty-eight hours.'

'It is possible.'

'My God,' she breathed and laughed out loud. 'Which means I shall be free—and you and your boss will be under arrest. Because my first port of call will be the nearest police station to press charges.'

'Your attitude may have changed by then.'

She said crisply, 'Not a chance, *signore*.' And paused, as a thought occurred to her. Be proactive, she told herself, instead of reactive. Test his loyalty to this unseen aristocrat.

She took a deep breath. 'Unless, of course, you're prepared to get yourself off the hook and do a deal.'

The dark brows rose. 'What precisely are you suggesting?'

So, she wasn't being dismissed out of hand, Maddie thought, exultancy stirring within her.

'That if you let me go in the morning—drive me back to Genoa, I'll say nothing about all this. No police, no charges, no jail. My silence in exchange for my freedom. What do you say?'

'I say—that it is not much of a deal.' He looked

her over slowly, his eyes lingering cynically on her mouth, and the swell of her breasts under the lapels of the robe. His insolent smile seemed deliberately to graze her skin. 'Have you nothing else to offer?'

It was suddenly difficult to breathe. And useless to pretend she did not understand. She steadied her voice. 'I—I thought you said that I did not attract you.'

He shrugged. 'This is an isolated spot,' he drawled. 'My choice in such matters is, of necessity, limited. So I am open to temptation.'

'But I am not,' she said between her teeth. 'Because you disgust me, and I hope you rot in jail forever, you bastard. I shall tell the authorities everything about this—House of the Wolf and the wolves that run it. The story will hit the headlines worldwide.'

He said quietly, 'I fear you will find the outcome rather different.'

'You're the one who should be afraid.' She pushed her chair back and rose shakily. 'It was a bad day for the Count when he decided to cross swords with Nigel Sylvester. He'll be sorry he was ever born for keeping me here, I swear it.'

There was a silence as their glances clashed—anger and defiance meeting faint amusement—and something far less easy to define.

At last he spoke. 'For once, Maddalena, I suspect you could be right. Now, run away to bed before I am tempted to reconsider your offer.

'And do not ask me what I mean,' he added softly. 'Because that is something we both already know. So do not annoy me by playing more games. Just—go.'

And Maddie found herself obeying him, walking to the stairs with all the dignity she could muster, holding up the skirts of her robe so she didn't stumble, trying to steady the judder of her heart against her ribcage.

As she reached the gallery, she found she was glad of Domenica's stolid presence waiting for her, and, above all, relieved that her strange prison cell possessed one door that would lock.

CHAPTER FIVE

TODAY, THOUGHT MADDIE, staring sightlessly out of the window. Surely it has to be today. It's got to be.

Because it should have been yesterday. Or the day before. Or the day before that. In fact, I was so absolutely certain it would be that I kept waking in the night, imagining I heard Jeremy's voice. But it was either a dream. Or wishful thinking. Or more probably a nightmare, because I'm sure at some point he called me 'Maddalena'.

To her annoyance, she felt her face warm, and her hands tightened on the windowsill.

But I won't let myself think about that, she told herself firmly. Because I will be free, even if it is nearly a week later than I hoped. Which is nothing really. Flights can be a problem, let alone transferring large sums of money at zero notice.

She sighed and turned away. The mountain view was no more welcoming now than the first time she'd seen it. While the second window she'd found at the other end of the room looked down on a small enclosed courtyard, apparently unused.

What she'd been allowed to see of the house itself told her it was large, but gave her no real idea of its layout, or how many people lived in it, apart from the Count and the jailer he employed to watch over her.

Andrea, she thought, her throat tightening as an image of him swam, uninvited, into her mind. A predator, as dark and dangerous as the wolf this house had been named for. Her enemy, himself as much of an enigma as the reason she'd been brought here.

Someone it was best not to think about, she told herself, returning to her original musings. Presumably, she would be taken somewhere else for the handover, and probably blindfolded so she couldn't report back on her temporary jail, and why she'd been shown so little of it.

She seemed to be shut away in a forgotten corner, and sometimes she felt that even if she could open any of the other doors that surrounded her, she would find they all led nowhere.

Stir crazy, she thought, with a sudden shiver. That's what's wrong with you, lady, and the sooner you're out of here the better.

She climbed on to the bed and stretched out, disposing the folds of her robe and nightgown around her. These were in a wonderful shade of amethyst, while yesterday's set had been deep ruby, with others in turquoise and indigo. In different circumstances, this would have been spoiling to the nth degree, and she wondered, smiling, what Jeremy would make of these dramatic jewel colours in clinging satin and the additional sheen they seemed to give to her hair and skin, suggesting she might actually rethink her trousseau a little.

As for tomorrow's choice—well, hopefully, I shall never need to know, she thought, crossing her fingers.

Yet the Count who'd paid for all this charming nightwear had never seen any of it. And she'd given up on the hope of seeing him too. She'd even stopped asking for him, as it was clearly a waste of time and temper.

So, let him behave like the Invisible Man, she told herself defiantly. He's simply ashamed to face me, that's all. Mortified to have to acknowledge what he's done. And whatever happens to him, he has only himself to blame for abandoning me to his henchman, who has no finer feelings to lacerate.

Not that she'd been much in his company either, except at dinner, where she was no longer alone with him, thank Heaven.

A manservant in a neat dark suit called Eustacio, who spoke a modicum of English, now served them at table and poured the wine, and the smiling maid whose name, Maddie had learned, was Luisa, assisted him.

While the meals generally took place in near-silence. No discussions on opera or anything else, and a return to strictly formal terms.

Maddie wouldn't permit herself to ask if there was any news from London. Because to appear anxious would allow him a minor victory in the unspoken war between them, which seemed to assume an extra dimension each time they met, no matter how little was said.

The memory of those final exchanges between them on that first evening was always with her, like an unhealed wound. As was the fact that he hadn't made the slightest attempt to apologise since.

And her continued lack of conventional clothing only added to her mental discomfort.

She sighed. She supposed she really should have made more effort to find some way out of her predicament. After all, it was pretty spiritless, lounging around in a negligee, however glamorous, waiting to be rescued. On the other hand, it wasn't exactly ideal attire for a fugitive either. He was right about that, she thought bitterly.

But unless one of the staff could be bribed, her chances of getting hold of something less noticeable seemed less than zero. And when she wasn't actually locked in her room, she was always under scrutiny.

But, as a cell, it was now a little more comfortable than it had been. For instance a pretty brocaded armchair had suddenly appeared to stand beside the courtyard window, and there was also another larger table where she ate her breakfast and usually her lunch. Today's had been a warm chicken salad, followed by a wonderfully rich pasta carbonara, and a tiny filigree basket filled with strawberries. This had been accompanied by a small carafe of white wine, and the inevitable coffee pot.

Whatever else, she had no complaints about the food, she admitted. And her imprisonment had become slightly more stimulating too, because, on her second night, she'd swallowed her pride and asked if she might at least have the book she'd bought at the airport returned to her.

'I wouldn't want to affect your negotiations by dying of boredom,' she'd added sweetly.

She'd received a stony look, but he had silently inclined his head, and the thriller in question was on her bedside table when she went upstairs.

And last night, as she'd risen and bade him good-night, he'd said to her amazement, 'You may borrow more books from the Count's library, if you wish. Domenica will escort you there to make your choice.'

'Oh.' Maddie hesitated. 'Well—thank you. But couldn't someone else do that?'

His brows lifted. 'Why?'

She shrugged. 'I don't find her particularly congenial.' *Which was putting it mildly. The girl seemed to radiate resentment and disapproval.*

'It is not essential that you should,' he said. 'What matters is that her family has served the Valieri faithfully for years.' He added coldly, 'I remind you of this in case you are considering the offer of another deal.'

Leaving her to retreat upstairs fuming.

And, once back in her room, to wonder why his boss had decided to make such a concession at this particular time.

Unless, of course, he was hoping some slight act of kindness and consideration on his part might persuade her to speak on his behalf at some future point. If so, he would be severely disappointed.

He is Crime. I am Punishment.

I never realised before that I could be so vindictive, she thought. But perhaps I never had sufficient cause.

She was roused from her reverie by the sound of voices outside and the rattle of the key in the lock. The door opened and Domenica came in, lips pursed in annoyance, accompanied by the girl from the kitchen who'd come for the lunch tray.

She looked flustered today, a strand of dark hair escaping from her cap, and a faint pink stain like fruit juice smudged right across the front of her white overall.

Maddie deduced from the brief exchange that it was the girl's less than pristine appearance that had aroused Domenica's disapproval.

Domenica handed the girl the tray, then turned to Maddie. 'You wish for books, *signorina*?' she enquired without enthusiasm. '*Andiamo.* Let us go.'

She chivvied the kitchen girl out of the room, with Maddie following. Halfway along the corridor, she paused, nodding at a door and giving some terse instruction.

As the door opened, Maddie could see over Domenica's shoulder that it was a storeroom for household linen, but that one section of the floor to ceiling shelving seemed to be devoted to staff uniforms. There were the neat black dresses and pretty organdie aprons worn by the maids, and next to them, grey and scarlet waistcoats, dark trousers and white shirts which suggested there were indeed male indoor staff, even if she'd never seen them.

Maddie wondered caustically if Andrea the Thug came here for his gear and decided it was unlikely.

There were rows of shoes and boots too, but the largest section by far was occupied by the starched white coveralls and caps for the kitchen staff, where the hapless girl, now sniffing a little, was making her selection.

Maddie turned away, tightening her sash. Clothing, she thought, biting her lip. Heaps of clothing behind an unlocked door offering a perfect disguise, and only a matter of yards away. If only she'd known. Yet what could she have done? Broken down her own door to reach it?

Besides, it hardly mattered now. Not when she was leaving anyway.

She heard the storeroom door close again. When the girl had disappeared, she said quietly, 'Weren't you a little hard on her?'

Domenica shrugged. 'She is *sciatta*. Untidy. His Excellency would be angry to see her wait on you so.'

'But he hasn't,' Maddie pointed out. 'He didn't.' *Because he's never around, as I know to my cost.*

Domenica's mouth curled. 'His Excellency sees everything.' Her tone brooked no argument, while her expression suggested that Maddie should mind her own business.

When they reached the gallery, Domenica ignored the staircase descending to the *sala* below, leading the way instead to the far end where another archway waited with a narrow corridor beyond.

They appeared to have reached a dead end, but Maddie was beginning to know better and was unsurprised when the stone wall ahead turned out to be another door.

It would take a ball of string to find my way out of this labyrinth if the opportunity ever occurred, she thought ruefully, as she was conducted down a winding flight of stone steps. *Thank God I won't need one.*

At the foot of the steps, the passage divided. In one direction, Maddie could hear the distant sound of voices and the kind of clatter that indicated the kitchens. In the other, there was yet another curtained archway waiting to change into a door.

Maddie's head was beginning to spin as they passed through into a wide corridor. Halfway down, Domenica paused and knocked on a pair of double doors which, by some miracle, were exactly what they seemed.

A man called, '*Entrare,*' and she opened one of the doors and stood aside to allow Maddie to precede her into the room. It was large and square, every wall apparently lined with books just as you'd expect in a library.

But, she thought, she was taking nothing for granted any longer.

Because the voice had already warned her who was waiting for her, wearing a blue denim shirt and pants today, and seated behind a massive desk, his dark head bent over the letter he was writing, his hand moving smoothly across the paper.

Cream paper, she saw. And black ink. Both of them horribly familiar. As was the handwriting...

Maddie's lips parted in a silent gasp. I should have guessed, she thought wildly. Should have known. Because nothing is as it seems in the House of the Wolf. Nothing—and no-one.

Without looking up, he said, 'Take a seat, *signorina.*'

'Shouldn't I remain standing?' she asked bitterly. 'Your Excellency?' She added, 'Now who's the one playing games?'

He shrugged a shoulder. 'I realised you would have seen the late Count's portrait at the Opera

House, and found the temptation to conceal my identity irresistible.'

'Yes,' she said. 'That's what this place is all about. Deception and pretence. Why stop at a few painted walls?'

'If you wish to see it like that.' He gave her a cold smile. 'But I had other reasons. You can tell much about someone from the way they treat their supposed inferiors.'

'I didn't think of you as inferior,' she said, stonily. 'Just as a blackmailing criminal. I still do.'

'Unfortunate,' he said. 'When you and I, *mia bella,* are destined to continue to enjoy each other's company for a while.'

She said slowly, 'You mean I'm *not* leaving yet? But why? What's happened?'

He signed his letter. Blotted it. 'There has been no contact from your *fidanzato*'s family.' His voice was as cool as if he was telling her that rain was expected. 'It seems your immediate release is not their first priority, and they are considering their other options.' He paused. 'Such as they are.'

'I don't believe you. You're lying.' Her voice rose. 'Jeremy would never leave me here like this. You don't understand.' She banged her fist on his desk. 'We're going to be married—very soon.'

'*Sì*,' he agreed almost casually. 'In six weeks.

However, I expect this matter to be settled before then.'

She said hoarsely, 'What makes you think that?'

'I have stated my terms. All they need do is accept them.' He lifted his hands. 'It is simple.'

'Not where Nigel Sylvester is concerned.' Her voice shook. 'You don't dictate to a dictator, *signore*.'

'No,' he said. 'You defeat him in battle.'

'No matter what happens to the innocent parties involved?'

'Ah.' He leaned back in his chair, his gaze reflective. 'You refer to yourself? But I have removed you from the conflict.'

'But perhaps I don't want that.' She glared at him. 'Maybe I want to be with the man I love, fighting at his side.'

'Then you will be disappointed.' He indicated a table at the other side of the room, where an open cardboard box was waiting. 'And there is a selection of English books for you, to pass the waiting time more pleasantly.'

'Damn you,' Maddie said fiercely. 'And damn your books. I want nothing from you.'

'Now you are being irrational,' the Count said calmly. 'I will have the books taken to your room. If you choose to throw them down the mountain side, *naturalmente,* you may do so. But if your *fidanzato*'s family prove obdurate, you may regret it.'

'And please stop calling him by that outlandish name,' Maddie flared. She was beginning to tremble inside as the full horror of her situation dawned on her. They couldn't intend to leave her here indefinitely—they couldn't... Could they?

She added, 'He's Jeremy.'

Say his name. Conjure up his face in your mind—his voice. Hang on to every wonderful memory you've shared and believe that you'll see him soon—very soon.

'And I am Andrea,' he drawled. 'A name that you are reluctant to use—Maddalena.' He was watching her through half-closed eyes. 'I know now that the photograph of you I was once shown did not do you justice, *mia bella.* It made you look *convenzionale*—even a little dull.'

He nodded slowly. '*Sì*, passion suits you. It gives fire to your eyes and colour to your skin. What a pity I have so far only seen anger have this effect, turning the serene English rose into a tigress.'

She clenched her fists in the skirts of her robe, forcing herself to breathe calmly and evenly. To regain some measure of control.

'Please don't imagine I find your offensive remarks flattering, *signore.* Or that I intend to listen to any more of them.'

His mouth curled in amusement. 'What is offensive about telling a woman that arousal makes her beautiful?' He paused. 'Has this man—this Jeremy never told you so?'

'My relationship with him is no business of yours.' Maddie lifted her chin. 'And now I am going back to my room.'

'I shall not stop you.' He reached for his pen. 'For one thing I have other letters to write. For another—the time is not yet right.' He added quietly. 'But that will change.' And looked up at her.

Their gazes met. Clashed. Became caught in a new and tingling awareness. Making her conscious that there were golden flecks in his eyes, like tiny flames, dancing.

Maddie, shocked, found she had to force herself to look away. She said raggedly, 'Never—do you hear me? Never in a million years.'

She whirled round in a flurry of amethyst silk and stormed to the door, flinging it wide, startling Domenica, who was waiting outside with her arms folded.

She set off, almost running, in spite of the fact that her legs were shaking under her, desperate to reach the nearest thing to safety that she had in this chaotic dangerous world that held her trapped.

And she fought back the stricken tears already pricking at her eyes and aching in her throat.

Yes, she wanted to cry—to scream—to beat on the walls with her fists. But for all those things, she needed to be alone where no-one could see and mock her distress. Or realise how alone and isolated she felt. Or how scared she was—mostly for reasons she did not even want to contemplate.

So, she would break down in front of no-one—especially Andrea Valieri and his sour-faced spy, now struggling to keep up with this headlong dash.

When she reached her door, she flung it open, marched in and kicked it shut behind her. She half-expected it to open again to admit Domenica with the shrill tirade she was sure had been burning on her lips, but there was only a long silence, followed by the sound of the key turning in the lock. Something that, for once, she welcomed.

She threw herself across the bed, her fingers digging into the coverlet, and buried her face in the pillows as the first harsh sob rose in her throat.

Now that the tears had come, they were scalding, uncontrollable, and she welcomed that too, sensing somehow that she was weeping away all the tensions and fears that she'd been trying to suppress since this nightmare began.

That this was a catharsis that she needed.

When the storm passed, she felt limp and empty. She sat up slowly, pushing the damp strands of hair away from her face. She had to think about this latest development, she told herself, and think clearly too.

She'd been counting too much on other people. Taken it for granted that instant aid would be on its way, and that freedom was a foregone conclusion.

She took a deep breath. Well, she knew better now. And one of the uncomfortable facts to be faced was that Nigel Sylvester might indeed refuse to rescue her, regarding it as her own wilful disobedience that had led to this predicament in the first place.

'She put her career before you,' she could hear him saying to Jeremy. 'As she always will. And this is where it's led. She'll never make the wife you need and deserve, and it's time you came to terms with this. Admitted that marrying her will never work.

'Besides, she won't come to any real harm. When the kidnappers realise we have no intention of giving in to their demands, they'll have to let her go.'

In return, Jeremy would protest that he loved

her, that she was the girl he wanted. Of course he would. But his hands were tied. His father controlled the money, and there was no way he alone could raise the kind of ransom being demanded. Whatever that was.

I wonder what I'm valued at in hard currency, she thought bitterly.

Even so, whatever the terms of her release, she knew that Nigel Sylvester would still see her as a liability, and do his best to have the wedding postponed at the very least.

Therefore, she could no longer afford to let matters drift. Somehow, she had to seize the initiative and try to engineer her own escape.

There were elements on her side. She knew now where there was a change of clothes that might prove an adequate disguise, and she had seen more of the house, including where the kitchens were sited. It might not be much, and there was still this locked door to be dealt with, but it was a start.

She would not allow Andrea Valieri's scheming to threaten everything she held dear in life, she told herself, her heart jolting painfully.

But perhaps she was being unduly pessimistic. Maybe moves were already afoot to trace her secretly. To use some kind of professional negotiator, a fixer to arrange a compromise deal.

She had to believe that, in case her jailers were too watchful and self-reliance proved inadequate. Had also to pin her faith on Jeremy fighting for her. Coming to find her.

'Oh, darling,' she whispered brokenly. 'I need you so badly. For God's sake hurry.'

And just managed to stop herself saying, 'Before it's too late.'

CHAPTER SIX

As she showered away the signs of distress and weakness, Maddie decided that, to begin her campaign, she should try to regain some of the ground she'd lost earlier.

It had been unwise to lose her temper, and let him see how much this lack of response from London disturbed her. And sheer folly to over-react to his more personal remarks, she thought broodingly. Far better to have kept her cool and shrugged it off as trivial banter.

But from now on she would remain impassive in the face of any news, good or bad, and display total indifference to his sexual teasing. And if he persisted, she would tell him quietly that his behaviour was a breach of the good manners his birth entitled her to expect. Shame him into silence.

Although instinct warned her that he would not shame easily.

He would probably be anticipating more fireworks at dinner, but he would be disappointed, she thought as she dried her hair. She would conduct herself impeccably, speaking when spoken to and refusing to rise to any bait. And that's how it would be, however long she remained in this place.

At the same time, she would be looking all the time for a way out. Any chance, however slight, would do. And somewhere she would find help. There had to be a village around, albeit a small one, with communications to the world at large.

She wrapped herself in a fresh bath sheet and trod back into the bedroom for the siesta which had become part of her ritual. And when she awoke a new nightgown and robe would be waiting. As usual.

Emerald this time, I suppose, she thought as she stretched out on the bed. Although that's not my colour. I wonder if he'll realise that.

She bit her lip. That was not a train of thought, frankly, that she needed to pursue. He was hardly likely to have gone into some shop and chosen these frankly intimate garments himself. He'd have got some hireling to do so. But it was quite bad enough knowing that he'd given the order for her to spend her time dressed—or undressed—like this.

And if he'd seen her photograph, that meant he already knew her colouring and Heaven knows what other details about her, she thought, her face warming.

That was what she was finding so unnerving. All the research and planning that had gone into trapping her, of which she'd been so blithely unaware. The unseen power that this man—Andrea Valieri—had been able to exert to achieve it.

The feeling of helplessness, as if this deliberate removal of all her personal things had also wiped away her identity.

Added to that—the terrible realisation that she was merely a pawn in some game being played out by two arrogant men, and that pawns were easily sacrificed...

Stop that right now, she told herself with swift determination as a shiver curled the length of her spine. That's defeatist thinking and I'm not going to be a victim or a puppet any longer.

I'm taking my life back.

She slept eventually, and woke to a room full of evening shadows. As she'd expected, she'd had silent visitors while she was sleeping, and the new robe and nightgown were waiting for her, laid across the foot of the bed. But, this time, she discovered, they were black instead of the anticipated green.

Different styling too, she thought as she held

them up, frowning. The robe had a revealingly deep square neck and was fastened down the front with large buttons embossed elaborately in velvet. And the nightdress was made from chiffon so sheer it was hardly more than a thin veil, with only narrow ribbon straps supporting its tiny bodice.

Sending her, Maddie realised furiously, an unmistakable message. A sensuous offering with deliberate provocation in every inch of fabric.

Well, it won't work, she silently informed her unseen antagonist. I'll wear the damned things as if they were towelling and flannelette.

As she glanced around, she saw the box of books on the table, and lying next to it her CD player with the disc of Floria Bartrando's favourite arias.

Another concession, she thought, biting her lip uneasily. It was hardly a charm offensive, but it was disturbing just the same. Although it made no difference. Nothing he could say or do would ever change her attitude towards him. Her mind and her body were immune to his overtures.

He was her enemy, and, once she was free of him, he would suffer for the way she'd been treated.

If Jeremy didn't kill him first, she thought, viewing her reflection with disquiet. The robe's tight bodice enhanced the slenderness of her waist and showed far too much of the creamy swell of her breasts. While those buttons which were supposed to keep it fastened seemed much more invitation than protection, she thought, hating the sudden colour that flared in her face.

Tonight it was Luisa who came to escort her downstairs, her eyes and mouth round with astonishment as she looked at her.

Whatever you're thinking, you're wrong, Maddie muttered savagely under her breath, grabbing up the CD as she passed the table.

She was halfway along the corridor when she heard the music. A piano playing something soft and lilting—and not far away. She paused to listen, wondering, then drew a deep breath as she remembered.

He had lessons in childhood. Andrea Valieri's casual words. *Now he plays only for his own amusement.*

And doesn't he like to amuse himself, she thought scornfully, as she walked out on to the gallery. He doesn't miss a trick. What will it be next? Mandolin serenades under my window?

She stopped halfway down the stairs, looking down the length of the room, watching him, her hand resting lightly on the stone banister, her body taut under its light draperies.

And the music was certainly beguiling, played in

a minor key, dancing joyfully along one moment, wistful and plangent the next.

His dark head was bent over the keys. He seemed intent—oblivious, but she wasn't fooled. He was as aware of her as she was of him. Even at this distance she could feel it, like the stroke of a fingertip over her bare skin.

She realised, shocked that her nipples were lifting and hardening against the chiffon that cupped them. Recognised her body's desire to sway with the rhythm of the music. To let it take her down the stairs and towards him, the black silk floating around her.

Recognised it and fought it. So that when the final chord rippled into silence, she was able to applaud slowly, almost languidly, making him look at her directly. Letting him register the silent challenge of her pose.

'*Bravo, signore.*' She moved then, descending the remaining stairs. 'And I thought you said you weren't a virtuoso.'

He rose. 'Flattery from you, *signorina*?' he queried sardonically. 'I am astounded.'

'I think it would take a good deal more than that to surprise you.' She paused. 'I didn't recognise the music. What was it?'

'It is something quite new, composed by someone I was at school with, Gianfranco Deloria. He has been collecting old forgotten folk music from this area and giving it a contemporary twist.'

'Well, it's—beautiful.'

'He would be pleased to hear you say so. His first album is coming out quite soon, and he will give a recital in Trimontano in the autumn.'

'Ah, yes,' she said. 'The festival. Which reminds me—thank you for the return of my player, but you may keep this.' She put the Floria Bartrando CD on the dining table. 'I don't want any souvenirs of my time in this place.'

'And yet she is what brought you here.'

'As if I needed reminding.' She allowed a trace of bitterness in her tone. 'However, that's when I thought I was researching for a television programme. Now I doubt that Floria Bartrando still exists, let alone has plans to resume her career.'

'On the contrary, she is alive and well,' he said after a pause. 'And she does intend to sing again one day—when the time is right.'

'Then she'll do it without any help from me.' Maddie shrugged. 'Does she know you involved her in your scheming?'

'I would not have used her name without her permission.'

'So you do occasionally have scruples. Now I'm

amazed. And especially about Signorina Bartrando,' she added musingly. 'How can someone with the voice of an angel lend herself even marginally to an extortion racket? Has she fallen on hard times?'

'She lives in perfect comfort.'

'And so do you.' She glanced around her. 'Or have you been hit by the global economic downturn? Are the olive oil and ceramics markets heading for the rocks?'

His brows lifted. 'No, they are not. But your research has been thorough.'

'But clearly I didn't look deeply enough,' Maddie said. 'For instance, I found no mention of the late Count's death.'

'He wished it so,' Andrea Valieri returned. 'He was a very private man.'

'Then perhaps it's as well he's not here to see you drag his name through the dirt.' She sent him a challenging look. 'Or, like you, did he consider himself above the law?'

'No-one is that, *mia bella*.' His sudden smile touched her like a kiss, and she had to overcome the urge to take a step backwards. Because that would be a damaging act of self-betrayal that she could not afford.

But she could not control the faint breathlessness in her voice. 'Don't—call me that.'

'You think it is more deception?' he asked softly. 'I promise it is not.' The amber gaze studied her, lingering on her breasts then travelling slowly down the rest of her body as if he was imagining what he would see if the robe were gone. 'You were lovely before, Maddalena. Tonight you are breathtaking.'

'And stop talking like that.' Her words were falling over each other. *Stop looking at me. Stop standing only a few feet away. And, dear God, stop smiling as if you already knew—everything there is to know about me. Because that scares me far more than any number of hours in a locked room.* She rallied. 'You have no right—no right at all.'

'I have any rights I choose to impose,' he drawled. 'But there is no need for such panic. I was paying you a compliment, not attempting seduction.'

'Seduction?' She lifted her chin defiantly. 'Don't you mean—rape?'

'No,' he said with sudden harshness. 'I do not, and you insult me and the ancient name I bear by such a suggestion. Because I swear on the honour of my family, that I have never in my life taken a woman against her will.' He paused. 'And you, Maddalena, will not be the first.'

His eyes narrowed. 'If you are honest, surely you must know that? Or is it possible that you are still an innocent with no experience of how a man expresses his desire?'

'Of course not.' She took a deep breath, adjuring herself silently to get a grip. 'You know quite well that I'm engaged—and about to be married.'

He shrugged. '*Sì.* But one thing does not necessarily rule out another. And you seem—curiously untouched.'

'Curious indeed,' she said, crisply. 'As Jeremy and I are deeply and passionately in love. But I suppose I have to endure your unpleasant sexist speculations along with everything else you've inflicted on me.'

'That will not be necessary. I have already drawn my own conclusions about the depth of passion you have experienced.' He paused. 'But tell me, *mia cara,* have you never wondered if there could be more?'

'No.' She glared at him. 'Because loving someone and wanting to spend your life with them isn't all about sex.'

'Ah,' he said. 'A cynical man might say you had just condemned yourself, Maddalena.' He paused. 'So where is this devoted and passionate lover? If you belonged to me, I would be here, beating at the door, offering everything I possessed in the world to get you back into my arms. Except...'

'Yes,' Maddie prompted coldly. 'I'm sure there'd be an exception.'

'Except I would never have permitted you to travel into the unknown without me,' the Count said harshly. 'I would not have allowed you out of my sight by day and would have made sure you were safe in my bed each night. Why did he not do the same?'

Safe in *your* bed? thought Maddie. In what alternative reality would that be true?

'Jeremy has an important career.' She faced him defensively. 'He had other things to do than follow me round Italy.'

His mouth twisted. 'In other words, *mia bella,* he was obeying his father's orders. No, do not attempt to deny it,' he added as her lips parted indignantly. 'My research has also been thorough.'

'And, like mine, incomplete, because you don't know my future father-in-law,' she flashed back.

'Nor, Maddalena, does he know me. You seem to forget that.'

She moved a hand impatiently. 'Because it makes no difference.' She paused. 'Oh God, how can I convince you that he'll never give into your demands. I expect Interpol are searching for me right now.'

'I would not count on it,' he returned calmly. 'Nor should you.'

'I'm counting on one thing only,' Maddie said fiercely. 'Getting out of here damned quickly.' And managed, just in time, to stop herself adding, 'And as far away from you as it's possible to get without leaving the planet.' Because, although true, it was altogether too much of a revelation.

The sound of the door and the rattle of the trolley announced Luisa's timely arrival with the drinks, and Maddie turned away, drawing a relieved breath.

She was tempted to ask for mineral water, but instead accepted her spritzer without comment. Everything as usual, she thought, in spite of him.

When Luisa had poured him his whisky, she was quietly dismissed and they were alone again.

Needing a neutral topic of conversation, if there could be such a thing in these circumstances, she wandered towards the fireplace, taking a closer look at the oil painting that hung there.

'A strange subject for a picture,' she commented lightly. 'Is that the actual wolf the house was named for?'

'No, he was merely a symbol, painted from photographs. Originally, this house was called *Casa d'Estate*—the House of Summer. My great grandparents named it that because they spent their summers here to escape the heat of the coast.

'It was my grandfather who made the change. Forty years ago, studies revealed that the Apennine wolf was in danger of being wiped out. He had always found them interesting animals, brave loyal and with close family bonds, and he was among those who worked to protect them. They are now on the list of endangered species.'

Maddie frowned. 'But they're dangerous themselves, aren't they?'

He shrugged. 'To smaller animals, certainly. They are carnivores, *sì,* but they also eat berries and plants. My grandfather had to battle with local shepherds and the hunters who saw the wolves as trophies. He had the painting done and re-named this house to demonstrate to the world which side he was on.'

'That can't have made him very popular.'

'It did not. But to the local people he was the *padrone* and the Valieri have always been good landlords who did not ill-treat or exploit their tenants, so they grumbled but respected his wishes.'

He smiled reminiscently. 'And when people argued with him, he told them never to forget that the Roman empire owed its existence to the she-wolf who suckled Romulus and Remus.'

'And did they accept that?' Maddie found she was smiling too.

'Not for a moment,' he admitted. 'But it usually ended the debate. He was a very determined man.'

'A trait he has obviously handed down.' Maddie spoke lightly, and, to her surprise, saw his face change, harden.

'It may seem so,' he said, after a pause.

'Ah,' she said, hiding her surprise at his response. 'Could that mean that, even now, you might be open to persuasion? After all, you've made it clear you don't need the ransom money.'

'But it is not a question of money,' he said quietly. 'And never has been.'

She stared at him. 'What then?'

'I could tell you,' he said. 'But at present you are too hostile, too suspicious, Maddalena, to believe anything I might say. So explanations must wait for a more favourable time. As you must also wait for the Sylvesters' response. I wonder which will come first.

'And no persuasion you can muster, however tempting, will cause me to change my mind,' he added softly. 'So do not try.' He paused. 'Unless, of course, you are looking for an excuse to share my bed. Although that is not necessary,' he added musingly. 'I promise that "Andrea, I want you" is all you need say.'

They were several feet apart, but the atmosphere between them was suddenly charged—electric with tension.

Maddie's breathing quickened. She said unsteadily, 'How dare you insult me like this. It's disgusting.'

'Let me ask in return how you dare be such a hypocrite, *mia bella*,' he retorted, his mouth twisting cynically. 'I am simply acknowledging that the desire between us is mutual. Which you know as well as I do.

'Besides,' he added. 'The choice will always be yours.'

'Then I choose not to be alone with you again!' Her voice was stormy.

'You will have your wish,' he said calmly. 'At least for the next few days. I have business elsewhere.'

'More helpless people to kidnap?'

'I hope,' he said, the amber eyes glinting in that disturbing way, 'that you are not describing yourself in those terms, Maddalena.'

'But supposing there's a message from Jeremy

and his father, offering terms. You won't be here to get it.'

'Have no fear,' he said. 'If there is any break-through, which I doubt, I shall be informed.'

'But I shan't be,' Maddie protested furiously. 'I'll have to stay locked up here in total ignorance when anything could be happening.'

'You are still hoping perhaps that your future father-in-law will pull strings in Whitehall and have the British SAS parachute in to rescue you?' He sighed. 'A vain hope.'

'But there's another factor in all this that you've overlooked,' Maddie said tautly. 'The television company I work for, who sent me here. They're expecting regular reports on my progress with the Bartrando research. If they don't hear from me, they'll become concerned and start making en-quiries.'

'But they have received several texts from your mobile phone assuring them that all is going well,' he said gently. 'They will be disappointed if you eventually return empty-handed, but that is all.' He paused. 'Now that I have set your mind at rest, let us have dinner.'

'No thank you,' she said, putting down her half-empty glass. 'I'm going to eat in my room. Perhaps you'd arrange for someone to bring a tray. Some pasta and dessert will be fine. I'm not hungry.'

He shook his head. 'That is a banal reaction and not worthy of you, *carissima*,' he commented. 'But if that is indeed what you want, I will give the necessary orders. I shall also summon Domenica to escort you back.'

He went to the fireplace and tugged at the embroidered bell pull. 'However,' he continued, 'I hope you will continue to dine down here during my absence.'

She was already on her way to the stairs, but she turned looking at him almost blankly, as she recalled there were at least two exits from the room. 'You trust me that far?'

'No,' he said. 'But Eustacio will be here, and I trust him to look after you on my behalf.' He watched her bite her lip and added silkily, 'Besides, it will give me pleasure while I am away to think of your beauty gracing my table. And to imagine a time when we shall not part for the night once the meal is over.'

Sudden, helpless warmth flooded her face, and was echoed by the slow torment of the heat slowly uncurling inside her. The betraying sensuality of that deep inner ache, telling her unequivocally that all her protests were lies and how it would be all too easy to say 'Andrea—I want you', instead of the biting riposte which would silence him now and forever.

Her nails scored the palms of her hands, as, to her eternal shame, the words of angry dismissal failed to materialise.

And as she climbed the stairs towards Domenica's solid bulk in the shadows, she could feel the Count's gaze following her as if he were walking with her, his hand on her waist, and his lips grazing her hair.

And heard his voice, faintly mocking. 'Until we meet again, Maddalena. Believe me, *carissima,* I shall count the hours.'

And found herself praying silently that she would not do the same.

CHAPTER SEVEN

MADDIE READ THE last page of her book, sighed, and tossed it away from her. She swung herself off the bed and began to walk up and down the room in the mid-afternoon sun.

Andrea Valieri had been gone for two days now, and when she'd forced herself to ask Domenica when he was expected back, the other woman had shrugged with sour malice before informing her that the business which detained him was a girl in Viareggio. 'His *amante,*' she'd added unnecessarily. 'And very beautiful, so who knows when he will return.'

All the same, Maddie knew, with every hour that passed, that her chances of escape, already slim, were becoming positively skeletal.

Of course, he hadn't been serious about counting the hours until he saw her again. He'd simply been winding her up, and she knew that. Told herself so continually.

Nevertheless, the news about the girl in Viareggio had shaken her to the core, and she'd had to work damned hard to conceal her inner turmoil from Domenica's sly scrutiny.

She found herself wondering just how much the maid had heard and understood of the exchanges between her master and his prisoner while she was on escort duty and what deductions she might have made.

Another good reason for getting out of here, Maddie thought biting her lip with unnecessary savagery.

Because, if she'd been frightened before, she was now in a completely different kind of danger. And she was petrified.

She had spent the last forty-eight hours striving to convince everyone at the house that she was resigned to her fate, at the same time sticking resolutely to her decision not to dine or eat any other meal downstairs.

Eustacio had visited her that morning, looking anxious, to tell her His Excellency would be distressed to hear she had not left her room, even to pay another visit to his library.

'And I'm equally distressed at being made to stay here,' she'd returned quietly and he had retired, shaking his head.

She'd hoped, in Andrea Valieri's absence, that

there might have been a more relaxed attitude to her detention, but it hadn't worked out like that. Wherever he might be—and whoever he might be with, she thought, biting her lip hard, the Count's presence still loomed over the Casa Lupo, and she seemed to be watched more closely than ever.

Today's bright spot was that Domenica, the prison wardress, had so far not put in an appearance. No doubt busy making herself a new broomstick, Maddie thought bitterly. Though she was probably being unfair to a woman simply doing her job.

It was just the manner of it that was bewildering. Maddie was at a loss to understand why she was so unremittingly hostile. After all, the other staff weren't like that. Luisa and the girl from the kitchen, whose name was Jolanda, were always smiling and pleasant in spite of the language barrier, while Eustacio was courteous in the extreme.

Just a clash of personalities, I suppose, she told herself with another sigh. And while nothing could make her enforced stay agreeable, it would be easier if she was able to have a normal conversation sometimes with the person she saw most often.

And with that she heard the rattle of the key in the lock.

But it was again Luisa who led the way into the

room, carrying clean towels over her arm, followed by Jolanda who'd come, albeit belatedly, to collect the lunch tray, Maddie having finished her meal more than an hour before. She surveyed them in faint surprise. 'Domenica?' she queried.

The girls exchanged glances, then Luisa performed a brisk and realistic imitation of someone being violently sick.

'Oh,' Maddie said slowly. 'What a shame.' Then, remembering the scanty Italian derived from her phrase book, *'Che peccato.'*

The girls nodded then Luisa headed for the bathroom, while Jolanda picked up the tray and left the room with it, leaving the door open.

Maddie stared at it, swallowing. This was the first time it had ever happened. Domenica invariably locked the door as soon as she was inside it. But it might be the nearest thing to a chance she would get and she had to take it.

She took one uncertain step then halted as a shattering crash and a shriek of pain came from the passage.

Without further hesitation, Maddie ran out and found a sobbing Jolanda picking herself up from the floor amid a welter of broken glass and crockery.

She was nursing one hand in the other, a deep cut across the palm oozing blood.

Groaning inwardly, Maddie helped the girl to her feet, and examined the wound, which was clearly a nasty one. She heard a horrified squeak and turned to find Luisa standing behind her, mouth open.

'Get a towel,' she directed, and as the maid stared at her in bewilderment, she pantomimed drying herself.

When Luisa returned with one of the small linen towels, Maddie wrapped it tightly round the injured hand.

'Now take her downstairs to the kitchen. *La cucina,*' she added as she received another uncomprehending stare. 'She needs to go to hospital. *Ospedale,*' she reiterated. '*Presto.* Her hand may need a stitch.' She demonstrated the action of sewing which drew agonised yelps and cries of '*Santa Madonna*' from both girls and renewed sobbing from Jolanda.

'And I'll see to that,' Maddie went on crisply, seeing Luisa gazing in consternation at the mess on the floor. 'You take care of her. *Attenzione,* Jolanda.'

Luisa nodded distractedly and led the other girl away, an arm protectively round her shoulders.

As they disappeared from sight, Maddie released

her indrawn breath. Luisa would ultimately remember that the room had been left open with the prisoner free to roam, and she could only pray it would be later rather than sooner.

The keys were in the door, and to buy a few extra minutes, she locked the door from the outside. Picking up her skirts, she jumped across the debris of her lunch tray and ran to the store room. She picked out a white overall that approximated to her size, grabbed one of the elasticated mob caps and a pair of low-heeled black shoes. She stripped off her robe and nightgown, thrusting them, with the keys, into a hamper for soiled linen at the side of the room, then dressed swiftly.

The overall's starched linen felt coarse and uncomfortable against her skin, making her feel even more naked than usual. Something else that Andrea Valieri would eventually pay for, she told herself, struggling to fasten the buttons.

But at least she was covered, and beggars could not be choosers, she thought as she crammed her hair into the cap and pulled it down so that, hopefully, not a blonde wisp was showing.

Then, slipping her feet into the clumpy shoes, she set off along the passage, rehearsing the route in her mind, and listening all the time for the alarm to be sounded. She tiptoed along the gallery, through the arch and made her way to the false wall, feeling for the door handle.

When she reached the foot of the steps and the spot where the passage divided, she turned towards the kitchens, keeping close to the wall, head bent, not hurrying too much. Just another girl getting through the working day, anonymous in her uniform.

As she got nearer, she could hear the hubbub of excited voices, and, rising above them, the sound of Jolanda protesting tearfully. The volume doubled momentarily as a door opened and a man emerged, carrying a box of bottles and jars. He sent Maddie a brief, incurious look and went on down the passage.

My disguise works, she thought, her heart thudding. He must be going to the garbage bins, and all I have to do is follow him.

She maintained a discreet distance, watching as he rounded a corner, and was rewarded by the screech of hinges and a sudden influx of sunlight up ahead.

Not ideal when compared with the dimness of the passage. But her luck was holding, because when she reached the open doorway, he was nowhere to be seen.

Maddie stepped out into a walled courtyard

lined with outbuildings. There was a gate in the far wall—or was this just more *trompe l'oeil*—designed to trap her in another part of the house?

But there was no imitating sunshine and fresh air, she thought with relief as she sprinted across the yard. And the gate was real, its heavy bolts sliding open, and the heavy ring handle turning with well-oiled ease.

She squeezed through the gap, then closed the heavy timbers carefully behind her. No need to leave clues to her chosen exit.

For a moment she stayed still, controlling her flurried breathing as she attempted to get her bearings.

The mountain that she'd seen every day from her window was over to her left, grey, monstrous and impenetrable as it loomed over the valley at its foot. Straining her eyes, Maddie could see far below the gleam of water and the pale line of a road that followed it—leading where?

Well, to civilisation, presumably, by the most direct route. The obvious choice for someone who needed to get away fast. But too obvious. She would be spotted miles away on that long curving descent. And even more easily by anyone returning...

The alternative route lay straight ahead of her.

A rough track rising steeply into dense woodland which seemed to be composed mainly of chestnut trees. Not very appealing, dressed as she was, but at least the canopy of foliage would hide her as she travelled, and the thick trunks offer cover if necessary.

She started up the slope, pulling off the cap and stuffing it into her overall pocket. As she shook her hair loose, she silently cursed her unsuitable footwear. Better than going barefoot, she told herself, but only just.

Once safely in the shade of the trees, she paused again briefly to look back at her erstwhile prison. It was even larger than she'd supposed, not so much a house as a *palazzo*, with an imposing square tower at its centre, and she wondered if there were already faces at some of those innumerable windows scanning the countryside for a glimpse of her.

A great block of immutable stone, she thought, taking a last look over her shoulder, totally in keeping with its remote landscape, and certainly not her idea of a *casa d'estate*—a summer house. Its latter name, the House of the Wolf, suited it much better—as well as matching the character of its owner, she added with something of a snap, and plunged into the forest.

The path was narrow and heavily overgrown in

places, but still reasonably discernible, indicating it had once been in regular use. So it could lead eventually to a hamlet or at least another house where there might be a telephone.

She tried to maintain a steady pace but it wasn't easy with all the fallen branches and foliage underfoot, or with the ill-fitting shoes she was wearing. She could almost feel the blisters springing up.

In spite of the shade, it was hot, and she was already growing thirsty. Pity there'd been no bottled water in the storeroom, she mused, wondering how soon she'd find some sign of human habitation. She seemed to have been walking for at least an hour or more, but without her watch, how could she tell? Yet surely the sun was considerably lower than it had been when she set out?

But she'd find water soon, she assured herself. There were bound to be streams feeding the river she'd seen in the valley, and she'd just have to risk their purity.

She couldn't, however, estimate her progress. She was no great judge of area, and these woods could well spread for acres.

There'd been plenty of woodland walks near her home when she was a child, but none of them like this. The trunks of the trees were thick and twisted, like something from an Arthur Rackham illustration. She could almost imagine gnarled arms emerging to seize her as they'd done in a scary Disney version of 'Snow White' she'd watched when she was little.

Shut down the imagination and stick to practicalities, she adjured herself. They're just trees. The real nightmare is behind you. And you can't be caught and taken back—for every kind of reason.

The forest was full of noises too: the whisper of leaves above her in the faint breeze, the rustling sounds in the bushes that flanked her path indicating the unseen presence of what she hoped were very small and friendly animals, and the shrill calling of birds which ceased abruptly at her approach.

Like a tracking device, she thought, with a faint grimace, easing her shoulders inside the stiff constriction of the linen.

And then she heard another noise, louder and more alien than anything else around her. The sound of an approaching helicopter.

Maddie gasped, shading her eyes as she stared upwards through the tangle of leaves and saw the gleaming silver body passing almost directly overhead. The increase in volume from its engine told her all too well that it was coming in to land, and she knew, heart sinking, who was almost certainly on board.

Oh, trust Andrea Valieri not to have done the conventional thing and travelled by car, she raged inwardly. And why had it never occurred to her that Casa Lupo might have a helipad?

He couldn't possibly see her, in fact he would assume she was still safely his prisoner, but she suddenly felt as exposed as if she'd been tied naked across a rock in the sunlight.

And it wouldn't be long now before he discovered the truth, she thought, a knot of panic tightening in her stomach. And then, like a wolf, he would begin to hunt her down.

Not immediately, of course, she told herself, trying to be optimistic. He might well think that she was hiding somewhere in the house, until someone discovered her robe and nightgown and forced him to refocus.

All the same, the path no longer seemed a blessing, but quite the reverse. She tried to calculate how long it would be before he came to look for her, and how far she could get in that time and find some kind of shelter, but her head was whirling like the blades on the helicopter, and nothing made any sense.

'Maddalena.' Another trick of the imagination seemed to bring her name to her on the breeze, and she shivered uncontrollably.

She thought, 'I can't let him find me. I can't...'
And knew it was not simply the fear of being
locked up again that was driving her on with such
desperation.

Determinedly, she dismissed her aching leg mus-
cles and sore feet and quickened her pace. Inevi-
tably, the track began to climb more steeply, and
along with the forest floor debris, she also had
loose stones to contend with.

She wasn't in condition for this, she told herself,
panting as she paused to wipe the sweat from her
eyes. And before too long she'd be getting dehy-
drated, and seeing things.

If that wasn't happening already, because the
branch of a tree hanging down across her path
seemed in some weird way to be moving, and turning upwards as if it was climbing itself.

'I'm going mad,' she said aloud, then stopped
with a stifled cry as she realised what she was
watching was a large snake, recoiling itself on to
the tree limb above it.

A snake. For a moment, Maddie stood motion-
less, rigid with revulsion, then she flung herself
sideways into a bush. For a brief moment, she
was held there by twigs and thorns, until, with
the sound of snapping wood, the bush gave way

and she found herself rolling helplessly downhill in a welter of earth, leaves and stones.

She just had time to think, 'This is where it ends,' only to find her rush halted as she collided breathlessly with a fallen tree trunk. Gasping and choking for breath, she remained where she was, wondering how many bones she'd broken in those few crazy, terrifying seconds.

And when she did sit up, slowly and gingerly, her first act was to look cautiously round her in case the snake had followed.

'I didn't know Italy had such things,' she wailed inwardly.

She moved her arms and legs with care, but they seemed to be working reasonably well, so she hauled herself to her feet, using the fallen tree as a lever, and stood for a moment, wincing. She was scratched, grazed and would be bruised to-morrow, and she'd certainly twisted her ankle, but she'd managed to escape serious injury.

But she was damaged in other ways too. Two buttons were now missing from the top of her over-all, now covered in earth and leaf stains, while the left-hand side of its skirt had been ripped open from mid-thigh downwards, taking it, she realised wretchedly, to the edge of indecency.

She sat down limply on the trunk and, fighting

back her tears, waited until the worst of the shock had worn off and she'd at least stopped shaking. Knowing that she had to set off again and soon.

It was chillier now, reminding her that sunset could not be far off. And there was no way she wanted to be still in this forest at dusk.

Glancing around, she selected a suitable branch, using it as a walking stick to propel her back to the top of the slope. It might also be useful as a weapon, she decided, thankful that the snake was nowhere to be seen.

But there was no point in pretending she could pick up the old pace again. She felt a protesting twinge in her ankle at the very idea, so she was reduced to limping sedately, cursing her luck with every awkward step as she resumed the long and tricky ascent.

The forest was quieter now. Even the birds were oddly silent.

I probably frightened them away with the noise I made crashing down that hillside, Maddie thought, grimacing. Not to mention screaming at the snake.

At the crest of the slope, the track forked sharply, leading downwards in both cases.

Maddie paused, leaning on her improvised cane as she considered her options. The right hand path was marginally better kept, whereas the one on the left gave the impression it had been abandoned long ago. She had no coin to spin, so again she obeyed her instinct and ignored the more obvious choice.

She had been walking for about half an hour when the tangled greenery suddenly thinned out, and, her heart lifting, she saw below her in the sunset a cluster of stonework and slate roofs.

Houses, she thought, wanting to whoop with joy. People. I picked the right way after all.

She made her way carefully down the steep gradient, emerging into a village street lined with houses.

It was very quiet. No smoke came from the chimneys. No neighbours stood gossiping at their doorways. And as Maddie got closer she realised that most of the houses lacked doors and windows, and the slate roofs were sagging and in holes.

Whoever the inhabitants had been, they were long gone.

Except for one. A dog who came trotting out of an alley and stood in the middle of the street looking at her.

So where do you belong? Maddie wondered as she halted too. Because you're obviously not starving. So—take me to your master.

And then she looked again, and the beginning

of her smile faded as she realised exactly what she was seeing. As she recognised the size of the animal. Its colour and weight. And, most tellingly, the shape of its muzzle.

Remembering as she did so, the picture over the fireplace back at the house and its savage subject, here and now confronting her in the flesh.

Oh God, she whispered silently. Oh God help me.

She took a cautious, shaky step backwards, then another while the wolf watched her, unmoving, the yellow eyes intent.

A voice in her head was telling her to be steady— be calm. That she had a stick to defend herself and the last thing she should do was turn and run.

On which, she dropped the stick, turned blindly and ran, cannoning into the hard, strong body standing right behind her. Feeling muscular arms go round her, grasping her firmly. Inexorably.

'So Maddalena,' said Andrea Valieri with soft satisfaction. 'We are together again at last. What a delight.'

CHAPTER EIGHT

SHE COULD NOT even feel surprise. Just a trembling sense of the inevitable.

As he held her, she was aware of the scent of his warm clean skin, mingled with the musky fragrance of the cologne he used.

She felt something unfold inside her like the opening of a flower and began to struggle all the more, beating at his chest with clenched fists. But it was like trying to push over that damned mountain and his grip on her did not relax for an instant.

'Let go of me.' She gasped the words frantically. 'Oh God, can't you see? Are you blind or just crazy? There's a wolf…'

'There was,' he said. 'It has gone now.' He turned her to look back down an empty street. 'See?'

She saw. Realised also that she had escaped one predator only to fall back into the power of another, and that she had been living in a fool's paradise during these past few hours to think she could really get free of him. That he would not find her.

The Count held her at arm's length, surveying her frowningly. '*Santa Madonna*, what have you done to yourself?'

She could well ask him the same, she thought, dressed as she'd never seen him before in cord pants and long boots, and wearing what appeared to be a canvas jacket with an array of pockets over a dark shirt.

She lifted her chin defiantly. 'I had an accident. There was a snake hanging from a tree right in front of me, and I was terrified so I ran, and fell down a slope.'

He said tersely, 'My sympathies are entirely with the snake. Have you injured yourself?'

'Just my ankle.' Trying to run had been stupid and the joint was throbbing badly now.

He said something under his breath, then reached for her, swinging her up into his arms and carrying her towards one of the crumbling houses.

She began to struggle again. 'Put me down.'

'*Basta!* Be still.' It was an order not a request, and she subsided unwillingly against the strength of him.

As they neared the house, she saw that, unlike its neighbours, it had a door, even if it was no longer attached, but merely propped against an outside wall.

And as he carried her inside, she discovered it was furnished in a rudimentary manner with a table, two chairs, a sink served by a single tap, a fireplace and a decrepit stove. Also that, at the rear, an archway half-covered by a ragged curtain led to another room, equipped even more basically with a mattress on the floor.

She also noticed a large, serviceable backpack leaning against the wall, and next to it, a long case that quite clearly contained a gun.

He placed her on a chair and went down on one knee. 'Let me see your ankle.'

She jerked her foot backwards, stifling an instinctive cry of pain. 'Don't touch me.'

He gave her a long icy look. 'Attempting to escape was the act of a fool. Why compound your stupidity by refusing help that you clearly need?'

Oh, don't let him guess the reason. Please— please don't let him guess...

For a moment, she was silent, then she nodded as if defeated, and sat back, hurriedly dragging her torn skirt together over her bare thigh as he removed her shoes. He examined the blisters on her toes and heels, his mouth compressed into a hard line.

When he touched her ankle, his fingers were firm but gentle.

'There is no fracture,' he diagnosed eventually.

'I could have told you that,' she muttered, aware that her skin was tingling at his touch. Despising herself...

'Just a slight sprain,' he went on as if she hadn't spoken. 'It needs ice, but Giacomo has no freezer, so we must use what is available.'

'I didn't know you had medical training,' she said. 'In addition to all your other talents.'

'I don't,' he returned brusquely. 'Instead I have common sense. Permit me to recommend it.'

He looked her over again, frowning as she shivered suddenly, then stood up and went over to the fireplace, taking a box of matches from one of his jacket pockets and lighting the small pile of kindling in the hearth. Once it had caught, he added more wood from a sagging cardboard box, picked up a pot like a witch's cauldron and filled it at the sink before hanging it from a hook over the flames.

Then he went into the adjoining room, returning with a tin hip bath which he set in front of the fire.

Maddie drew a sharp breath. 'You have to be joking.' Her voice wobbled.

'No,' he said. 'Some of those scratches need attention, and must be cleaned first. But do not distress yourself,' he added with a faint curl of the lip. 'I shall not insist on witnessing the process.'

He opened a rickety cupboard under the sink, and produced some stubs of candles in chipped pottery holders, making her realise how quickly the light was fading

'Does this Giacomo actually live here?' she asked as he set the candles on the table, and lit them. 'He must find it lonely.'

He shrugged. 'He is a shepherd. He is accustomed to his own company, and he finds this place useful when he has sheep or goats to move.'

'And he doesn't mind visitors?'

'In this region, we help each other.' He looked at her with the first glimmer of a smile. 'It was Giacomo who told me he had seen you today and where he believed you were heading. Later Aldo, who was out looking for wild boar with his son, confirmed what he had said, and I came to find you.'

Maddie gasped. 'You mean I was being watched? All the time?'

'You think a blonde with hair like sunlight would not attract attention?' he countered, adding drily, 'The description is theirs, not mine. Besides, they were concerned for you. This is no country for someone without proper clothing or footwear.'

She bit her lip. 'Or anything to drink.' The admission cost her. 'I'm so thirsty.'

'*Dio mio.*' He cast a despairing glance at what was left of the roof before going to his backpack and producing a bottle of still water and a tin cup. 'Drink it slowly,' he cautioned as he filled the cup and gave it to her.

She sipped. 'But how did they let you know they'd seen me?' She added with constraint. 'After all, you were away.' *In Viareggio. With your mistress. Something that shouldn't matter because I'm in love with Jeremy—engaged to him—soon to be married. And I can't let myself forget that even for a second.*

And gulped some more water.

'I returned just as it was realised you were missing,' he said. 'And Giacomo and Aldo contacted me by radio.'

'Radio?' she repeated. 'Up here?'

'*Sì.*' He nodded. 'Hunting parties use them all the time to communicate with each other. The latest have a range of over ten kilometres.'

'How efficient of them,' Maddie said bitterly.

'It is for the best,' he said, shrugging again. 'You would not have wished to spend the night alone up here, even in surroundings as comfortable as this,' he added drily. 'What would you have done, *per esempio,* if you had found you were sharing your accommodation with a scorpion?'

She put the cup down. 'Is there one?' Her voice was hollow.

'No,' he said. 'But they often come in at night.'

'Scorpions,' she said unsteadily. 'Wolves. Snakes. It's a jungle out there.'

'It was probably a rat-snake if it was hanging from a tree.' He sounded infuriatingly casual. 'They are not particularly venomous, and prefer to crush their prey.'

'Wow,' she said. 'How fascinating. I only wish it had explained that to me before I ended up at the bottom of a hill.'

She paused. 'And how did you manage to get here before I did? You certainly didn't pass me on the way.' Otherwise, somehow, I would have known, she thought and controlled another shiver.

'There is another road,' he told her. 'Camillo left me there at the crossroads, and I walked across country to wait for you.'

'You mean the car's not far away?' She closed her eyes. 'Thank heaven for that.'

'You are so anxious to return to your jail?' He was pouring water again, this time into the bath using a jug from the sink cupboard, before adding the contents of the cauldron.

'On the contrary.' Her denial was instant, her tone defiant. 'But at least it's better than this.'

'I am glad Giacomo cannot hear you insult his hospitality.' He indicated the tub. 'Your bath awaits, *signorina*. I regret there is no soap or any towel. You will have to dry yourself on what you are wearing.'

She flushed. 'But that's impossible. It—it's all I have.' *As he knew perfectly well.*

He took off his coat, hanging it on the back of the other chair, then began to unbutton the charcoal grey shirt he wore beneath it.

She said hoarsely, 'What are you doing?'

'Calm yourself. I am not planning to join you in the bath.' He stripped off the shirt and tossed it to her. 'Wear this when you have washed.'

His skin was bronze, the sculpting of bone and muscle strong yet, at the same time, intrinsically elegant. His chest was shadowed with hair which arrowed down into the waistband of his pants.

Unlike Jeremy, whose skin was smooth and paler in spite of assiduous tanning. And whose shoulders were less broad. Less powerful...

She looked away hastily, dry-mouthed.

'I—I couldn't possibly...'

'Don't be foolish.' The amber eyes swept her. Lingered ironically. 'You will certainly find it more modest than what you are wearing now.'

Her face burned as she watched him walk to his

backpack, produce a thin wool sweater with a roll-neck and pull it over his head.

Finally, he took out a small jar and placed it on the table. 'Antiseptic cream,' he said, and disappeared into the street.

Swallowing, Maddie shed the overall, and stepped into the bath. It was one of the strangest she'd ever taken, but, whatever her misgivings, it felt warm and infinitely soothing as she sat, knees to chin, carefully washing away the smears of earth, before standing up and letting the water pour in small, blissful rivulets from her cupped hands down her aching body.

She kept a careful eye on the doorway, but there was not so much as a shadow to disturb her.

When she had finished, she turned the overall inside out and patted herself dry with the cleanest part. She applied the cream to the worst of her grazes, then, slowly and reluctantly, she picked up his shirt and put it on.

The scent of him lingered quietly in its folds, as potent as when he'd held her in his arms, making her fingers clumsy as she struggled with the buttons, fastening them from throat to hem.

He was right, she conceded unwillingly when she'd finished. Its covering was more than adequate—longer in fact than some of the dresses she'd worn recently in England. The sleeves hung over her hands, and she rolled them back to her elbows.

Then, taking a deep breath, she called, 'I've finished.'

But the immediate response she'd expected did not come. The doorway was filled only with the gathering darkness. Wincing, she ran to the door, peering out.

Calling, 'Andrea,' her voice high and urgent.

And saw his tall figure taking solid, reassuring shape among the clustering shadows as he approached.

'Is something wrong?' he enquired as he came up to her. 'Another snake, perhaps?'

'No.' She felt foolish. Angry too that she'd betrayed her vulnerability yet again. 'I didn't know where you were.'

'I took a walk,' he said, adding drily, 'As I am not a saint, I decided to remove myself from temptation.'

She knew she was blushing again, and was glad of the darkness.

She hunched a defensive shoulder. 'I—I thought the wolf might have returned. And you didn't take the gun.'

'Because there is no need,' he said calmly. 'You

are quite safe.' He put a hand gently on her shoulder, turning her back into the room. The warmth of his touch seemed to penetrate every bone in her body. 'Now, if you sit, I will attend to your blisters.'

She sat, hands folded in her lap, waiting while he carried the bath outside to empty it, before returning to the backpack and taking out a roll of bandage and a small tube.

'This is a gel,' he told her. 'It acts as an artificial skin.'

'Will it hurt?' My God, she thought. She sounded about five years old.

'A little,' he said. 'But it will help.' He added drily, 'I hope you heal quickly, *mia bella*. When I promised to return you undamaged, I had not bargained for how reckless you might be.'

Return you...

She said quickly, 'Is there news from London? Am I going home?'

'They have made no reply of any kind.' He was deft with the gel, but it stung all the same, giving her an excuse for the sudden tears welling up in her eyes.

She said huskily, 'And if they never answer, what will happen then?'

'You need not consider that,' he said. 'They will

respond eventually, I promise.' He put the cap back on the tube. 'You will have to be patient, Maddalena.' He paused. 'And take no more stupid risks,' he added as he began to strap up her ankle swiftly and efficiently.

'Oh, that's so easy for you to say.' She wiped away an errant tear with an angry fist.

There was a silence, then he said quietly, 'You will feel better, *mia cara,* when you have had some food.'

She rose. 'Then please take me back to the house. I'd prefer to eat in my cell—alone.'

'You will be very hungry by tomorrow,' he said. 'We will eat now.'

'Tomorrow,' she repeated, her voice rising. 'Tomorrow? You don't mean that. You can't imagine I'd spend the night here.' She didn't add, 'With you.' She didn't have to.

She saw his face harden. '*Purtroppo,* I fear that neither of us has any choice in the matter.'

'But Camillo brought you by car. You said so.'

'And I sent him back.'

'No.' Maddie's stomach was churning. 'No, I don't believe it. Why would you do that?'

'Because the road here, like the village, has been abandoned, and is dangerous. I would not ask Camillo to take such a risk in fading light.

'So he will come for us in the jeep tomorrow.'

He added bleakly, 'And you, Maddalena, must live with the consequences of your own foolishness.'

She sank back on to the chair. 'What's so foolish about wanting to be free?' she asked bitterly. 'To be back with the man I love?'

His voice was equally harsh. 'Nothing. But for the moment, there is only soup, bread and sausage. You may eat or go hungry as you wish.'

She sat, arms folded defensively round her body, watching his preparations. He added more wood to the fire, refilled the cauldron, coaxed the rusty stove to light, poured soup from a jar into a metal pan produced from his pack and set it to heat.

While it was doing so, he unrolled what she now saw was a sleeping bag attached to his pack, and took it into the other room. Maddie noticed uneasily that he was unzipping it completely and arranging it across the bare mattress as a coverlet. Turning it into a double bed.

She stiffened, feeling her heartbeat quicken. Oh God, no, not that…

Then she smelt the wonderful aroma coming from the stove, and her mouth began to water, rendering other considerations secondary, even if only on a temporary basis.

He shared the soup, thick with chicken, herbs and vegetables, between two tin basins, and brought it to the table with wooden spoons that had clearly been hand-carved, and a platter of bread and sausage cut into chunks with his hunting knife.

In spite of her apprehensions, Maddie ate every scrap put in front of her, and even managed a constricted '*Grazie, signore,*' when she had finished.

'*Prego,*' he returned laconically. 'And earlier you called me by my given name.'

So, he had noticed after all, she thought, vexed with herself.

She said shortly, 'A slip of the tongue. I was— nervous.'

'*Che peccato,*' he said lightly. 'My hopes are dashed once again.'

She kept her voice cool. 'Given the situation, you can't be hoping for very much.'

'No? But every man is allowed, surely, to dream.'

Instinct warned her that Andrea Valieri's dreams should remain strictly a no-go area.

She shrugged. 'Yes, if he has time to waste.'

'Yet don't you dream, *mia bella*, of the day, the hour, the minute when you will become a bride? And do you consider that a waste?'

Did she still dream, she wondered, startled, or had it all become swallowed up by swathes of fabric, floral decorations and place cards? Subsumed by the ongoing battle with Esme over every detail?

She couldn't be sure any more. Only certain that she wanted this conversation to stop.

Back at the House of the Wolf, she would have made some excuse and gone to her room. Here she did not have that luxury, and she was acutely conscious the only thing waiting for her was that mattress and its makeshift quilt. Which might well be waiting for him too.

She pulled herself firmly together. 'But my dream is coming true, *signore*. That makes a difference.' She paused. 'How is Jolanda's hand? Did it need stitches?'

'How good of you to ask,' he said mockingly, letting her know that the abrupt change of direction had been duly noted. 'It has already been attended to at the nearest clinic.' He added softly, 'A little drama, of which you took full advantage, *mia cara*.'

'Perhaps, but I can still be concerned. And I hope Luisa won't get into trouble for forgetting to lock me in.'

'She has been reprimanded.' He added grimly, 'And Domenica too will have something to say when she returns.'

'No surprise there,' Maddie said crisply. 'Does she really have to be so obnoxious?'

'She has another side. She is, *per esempio,* devoted to my mother.'

That startled her. 'Your mother's still alive?'

His smile, tender, affectionate, lit his entire face. Suddenly he was someone she had never seen before but wanted very badly to know, she realised, as her heart turned over.

He said, 'Very much so, I assure you.'

Oh,' she said. 'I—I just assumed...'

'Of course,' he said ironically 'Because to ask about my family, and use my given name would be to treat me as a human being, and it is easier to think of me as a monster.'

She looked down at the table. 'Hardly that. In spite of everything, you've been—kind tonight.'

'You are important to my strategy, *mia cara.*' His response was brusque again. '*Percio,* I cannot afford to let you go. Matters have gone too far for that.'

Too far, she thought, hazily as the candle flame seemed to swim in front of her eyes. But no further. She realised she was going to yawn, and tried to stifle it behind her hand, but, of course, he noticed.

'You have had a trying day, Maddalena. It is time

you went to bed.' His voice was expressionless. 'I regret the other facilities are only a hut outside the back door, but I have a torch.'

She said too quickly, 'I'll be fine right here.'

The dark brows lifted. 'Tired almost to death, *mia bella,* yet still fighting me? *Tuttavia,* I must insist. The mattress can easily accommodate us both, and I prefer to keep you beside me. I am sure you understand why.'

She said, stumbling a little, 'If I promise not to run away again, will you sleep out here?'

'No,' he said, adding with faint grimness, 'because, thanks to you, I too have had a wearing day, so you are in no position to make terms.'

Maddie got to her feet. 'But you said—you told me that you wouldn't do this. You promised.' She drew a swift sharp breath. 'I should have known I couldn't trust you—you bastard.'

'I said I would not take you against your will,' he corrected her. 'And I am in no mood to test your resolve tonight. I desire sleep, not pleasure.'

Her voice shook. 'You are—vile.'

'And you, *mia carissima,* are a painful and persistent thorn in my flesh,' he said harshly. 'Which I pray to God I shall soon be rid of.'

'Amen to that,' she shot back at him.

For a moment they glared at each other across

the table, then suddenly and unexpectedly he burst out laughing.

'Now we have said our prayers, Maddalena, we can indeed go to bed.'

He paused. 'Can you walk, or shall I carry you?'

The question hung in the air between them for what seemed an eternity. Her mind was suddenly empty of everything but memories—the strength of his arms—the scent of his skin. His smile...

So much that was best forgotten. That should never have existed in the first place. That she should have fought from the start with every atom of strength she possessed before it took her unawares. Turned her world—her certainties to chaos.

She said huskily, 'I—I can manage.'

'Then do so.' His tone was briskly impersonal. He went to his pack and retrieved the torch which he handed to her. 'I will clear up here and wash before I join you.'

She nodded wordlessly and made her way carefully into the other room. Thanks to the strapping, her ankle was not aching nearly as much, she thought as she braved the few feet of darkness beyond the narrow back door.

As he'd said, it was just a hut, and primitive was a compliment. Also she was unnerved by the rustlings and scratchings she heard all around her, which the wavering torchlight did not dispel.

She was almost glad to be back inside the house. The mattress was old and smelt of straw, but it was marginally better than the floor. She put the torch down beside her and lay for a moment, looking up at the stars which were plainly visible through the holes in the roof, trying to control her inner trembling. Waiting.

The candles in the outer room were extinguished, signalling his approach, and she turned hurriedly on to her side, seeking the furthest edge of the mattress, and digging her fingers into its sagging contours to avoid rolling off.

Her eyes were closed so tightly that coloured lights danced behind her lids, but she was fiercely aware of him just the same. Every sense telling her that he had come round to her side of the mattress. That he was standing above her, looking down at her. Oh God, bending towards her...

His voice was soft, its tone sardonic. 'I will take charge of the torch, *mia bella*. It occurs to me it is a heavy one and I have no wish to wake with a fractured skull. So now you may stop pretending and sleep well.' He paused. '*E sogni d'oro.*'

He moved away, and she felt the mattress dip under his weight. In spite of his assurances, she was rigid with tension, waiting for him to reach for her. But his only movement was to turn on his own side away from her, and a short while later, his deep, regular breathing told her that he at least had fallen asleep.

Slowly, gradually, she relaxed her grip on the mattress. She pillowed her head on her arm, breathing him again, as his shirt sleeve brushed her face, absorbing the male scent of him with a sudden, passionate hunger, which she could no longer dismiss or even deny.

The shame of it was corrosive. She'd known him only a matter of days, during which he'd been her jailer—her enemy. Anger and fear should have kept her safe. So why had nothing protected her from this strange turmoil of confused emotion?

I told myself I just wanted my freedom, she thought, her throat tightening. To get back to England, whatever the cost.

But it was never that simple. Because what I've really been doing is running away from myself. And from *him*.

And now there is nowhere left to go.

CHAPTER NINE

IT WASN'T EASY, as Maddie soon discovered, to lie wide awake next to a sleeping man, whom you were desperate not to disturb.

Especially when it was the first time she'd ever shared a bed for the entire night, she thought, wondering what would happen if her imitation of a statue was interrupted by an attack of cramp. Or sneezing. Or if she simply fell asleep and turned over…

Don't even think about it, she adjured herself grimly. Concentrate instead on the stars you can see through that hole in the roof.

But although her body was still, her mind remained restless.

Wasn't there some psychological syndrome, she wondered desperately, that caused victims to become physically attracted to their kidnappers?

Surely just knowing that would help her to fight this dangerous obsession. To overcome this bewildering, illogical need to move closer to the warmth of him, and the false security his arms seemed to offer.

Because she couldn't jeopardise her future—her marriage and all her dreams of happiness for what could only be a brief and sordid fling with a—a serial womaniser. A man, after all, who had spent the last two days and nights with another girl in some love nest in Viareggio.

A man who had surely done enough damage already to the Sylvesters, without enticing her—a promised wife—into this ultimate and disgraceful betrayal.

Think of Jeremy, she urged herself feverishly. Focus on him, and only on him. Think of being reunited with him, when all this will seem like a bad dream. Imagine being in *his* arms and belonging to *him* again.

At which point she paused, because, if she was honest, her sense of belonging had occasionally faltered in the past months.

And she found herself remembering unhappily how hurtful it had always seemed when Jeremy had dressed and left immediately after lovemaking, which had also been rushed and quite often less than satisfying—for her at least.

'You make me feel like a tart,' she told him one night while he was hurrying into his clothes. She tried to make it sound as if she was teasing rather than complaining, but he'd glanced at her defensively.

'Don't, darling. You know how things are.'

'Well, yes.' *Nigel Sylvester's shadow seemed to hang over them even in their most intimate moments.* She controlled a shiver, again, trying to sound jokey. 'But surely your father isn't having you watched.'

'Of course not, but he expects me to be first into the office each morning. So I need to leave from home.' He came over to the bed and kissed her. 'We'll soon be married, Maddie. We just have to be patient, that's all.'

And I have been, she thought now as she had then. In all sorts of ways. But for how much longer?

She looked back at the stars, trying, as a last resort, to count them, but always somehow getting the total wrong, and having to begin again. Until, eventually, she closed her eyes against their dazzle, and her mind to the numbers whirling in her head, and let sleep claim her at last.

The next time she opened her eyes, she saw above her a patch of sun-brightened blue sky signalling morning.

For a brief moment, she struggled to figure out

where she was or what had woken her, and then, destructive as a tidal wave, memory came rushing back, and slowly and carefully, she turned her head.

Andrea Valieri was lying less than a foot away from her, propped up on one elbow, his mouth curving in a faint smile as he watched her. The sleeping bag had slipped down from his body, revealing that, apart from a pair of silk shorts, he was all bronzed skin. His hair was tousled, and he needed a shave, but neither of those circumstances detracted one iota from his sheer physical appeal.

'*Buongiorno.*' His voice reached her softly. '*E come stai?*'

Dry-mouthed, Maddie stared at him, trying to make her voice work, and at the same time wondering what in the world she could possibly say...

He tutted reprovingly. 'Have you not learned how to respond when the man in your bed wishes you "good morning"? Then permit me to show you.'

He moved then, reaching out to scoop her closer as he bent and let his mouth brush hers.

It was the lightest of touches, but all the same Maddie was aware of it in every inch of her skin, every nerve-ending. But most of all in every pulse of the soft inner trembling building inside her.

A trembling which could so easily become an ache—which she could not afford.

Only to feel her resolve slipping away as Andrea kissed her again, his mouth moving on hers, still gently but with a growing insistence as the seconds lengthened into minutes.

Maddie felt the flicker of his tongue probing her lips, searching for the inner sweetness they protected. At the same time his fingertips were stroking back the damp, dishevelled hair from her forehead, then tracing the contours of her face down to the curve of her throat where they lingered.

Her breath caught in mingled apprehension and excitement as his lips followed the same path softly kissing her eyes, her cheeks, the tremulous corners of her mouth, before feathering his lips over the pulse in her throat, making it leap in anticipation.

When, at last, he raised his head, Maddie's face was burning, forcing her to stifle a gasp as she registered the sudden tumult in her blood.

Now was the moment—if ever—to push him away. To hang on to some atavistic notion of survival and test his given word that he would not force her.

She was not a virgin but, at the same time she

felt so inexplicably nervous and insecure that this might indeed have been her first time with a man.

Her body seemed to belong to a stranger, its reactions, responses to his mouth and hands, alien and bewildering, as if she was balanced on some brink as enticing as it was dangerous.

But when her hands lifted to his chest, it was not in the planned rejection. Instead, she found her fingers splaying across the muscular hair-roughened warmth of his torso, her palms pressing against the harsh thud of his heartbeat, knowing it echoed her own.

And as if responding to some unspoken invitation, Andrea sought her mouth again, his kiss deepening into passion, commanding a response, gathering her closer, as her lips parted at last to grant him the access he wanted.

And offer the surrender that she herself craved. No right—no wrong any more, she realised dazedly. Just this man and this moment. She could deny it no longer as she relinquished—released every pent-up sensation born of the tension that had been building between them since their first meeting.

Her nipples were pebble-hard under the concealment of her only garment, desire scalding between her thighs as their mouths explored and clung with heated, hungry delight. As their tongues met— mated in rising sensual urgency.

Eventually, Andrea lifted himself away from her, putting her back on the mattress, before leaning over her to unfasten, button by button the shirt she was wearing, his hand travelling downwards without haste, pushing the edges of the fabric apart so that his mouth could follow the warm, naked path he'd created, and seek the soft roundness of her uncovered breasts.

Maddie stroked the tangled black hair, her eyes closing as she savoured the delicious rasp of his chin against her bare flesh. Gasping with the pleasure that lanced through her as he cupped her breasts and raised them to his lips, capturing the dark-rose of each excited nipple in turn, and suckling them with delicate eroticism.

She could feel through the silk of his shorts the scorching strength of his arousal pressing against her, and her loins ached with the need to have all the male power of him sheathed inside her. To give herself completely.

But as her fingers sought his erection, Andrea halted her.

'Not yet, *mia bella*,' he told her huskily. 'For now I wish this pleasure to be for you.'

He unfastened the remaining buttons, and, for

a long moment, looked down at her naked body, his eyes glowing like molten gold. He moved so he was kneeling at her feet, lifting them carefully to his gentle kisses, while his hands stroked her slim legs, sliding them beneath her to caress the sensitive area at the back of her knees, sending a long shiver down her spine, before travelling up to her flanks and slowly and sensuously moulding the swell of her buttocks.

Then his hands firm and purposeful, he lifted her towards him, letting his mouth drift enticingly over her slender thighs, before he reached the soft shadowing between them and kissed that too.

Maddie made a little sound between a sigh and a whimper and heard him murmur, '*Sì, carissima,*' as if he was answering some question she could not find words to ask.

He parted her legs, his fingers exploring her, pushing into the hot, sleek wetness of her. Seeking the tiny, tactile mound of her clitoris and teasing it with a fingertip to aching, quivering arousal, before bending his head, and possessing her with his mouth, his silken tongue flickering on her at one moment, then circling slowly and voluptuously the next.

Making her moan and writhe as he slowly and

wickedly increased the exquisite pressure, coaxing her with devastating expertise towards her release.

She could hear a voice she hardly recognised as her own sobbing, 'Oh God, there—please. Yes—yes—now...'

And as her driven body finally reached the utmost pinnacle of pleasure and throbbed into climax, she cried out his name in joy and astonishment.

Afterwards, they lay wrapped in each other's arms, Andrea murmuring to her in his own language between kisses.

Nothing, she realised in wonderment, had prepared her for this moment. Had warned her of how he might make her feel, or the overwhelming sensations he would be able to exact from her eager flesh. She'd never denied she was capable of the normal female responses, but Andrea's lovemaking had taken her to a different dimension, quite outside any past experience. And her instinct told her this was only the beginning.

He'd truly said this time had been for her, she thought, her body still tingling in the aftermath of her delight, but now she wanted to pleasure him in turn.

Or as well, she amended, smiling against his skin

as she asked herself, astonished, how she could possibly want him again so soon.

He said softly, 'I have marked you a little, *mia cara,* I should have shaved. I will do so next time.'

She stroked his chin with the back of her hand. 'It doesn't matter.' And next time, she thought, was now...

She raised herself a little, leaning on one arm, then reached down, her fingers playing with the waistband of his shorts, deliberately tantalising him before she began to ease them down over his hips. And Andrea laughed softly, lying back in acquiescence, his arms linked behind his head, his whole attitude an invitation to take—or give— whatever she wanted.

And then between one breath and the next, everything changed. Andrea was no longer relaxed in sensuous anticipation, but jack-knifing into a sitting position, head bent as if he was listening for something.

'What is it? What's the matter?' Surprised, Maddie sat up too. He silenced her with a gesture and then she heard it. The distant blare of a vehicle's horn, succeeded by the faint noise of its approaching engine.

'Camillo,' he ground out. '*Dio mio,* I did not expect him so soon.' He pushed himself up from the mattress, jumping to his feet, and raking a hand irritably through his hair.

'Stay there,' he directed abruptly, heading for the outer room. 'I shall dress and deal with him.'

In spite of the curtain which he'd tugged into place as he left, she had a perfect view of Andrea, once more discreetly clad in his cord pants and sweater, moving the barrier from the doorway and walking out into the sunshine.

Leaving her there in a tangle of mixed emotions, with disappointment, embarrassment, and physical frustration leading the pack, as with unsteady fingers, she tried to fumble the shirt buttons back into their holes under cover of the sleeping bag.

Knowing that having tasted rapture in his arms, she'd wanted the full banquet. And that she should be relieved that Camillo had signalled his approach and not caught them *in flagrante*.

And stopped right there, the breath catching in her throat. What was she thinking of? she asked herself incredulously. Because she had other far more cogent reasons for welcoming the interruption.

I nearly made the biggest mistake of my life, she thought frantically. Oh God, how could I have been so stupid?

Yet, if she was honest, she knew exactly why.

The plain fact was she'd been subjected to the attentions of a practised seducer, and, in spite of all her brave words and pious resolutions, she hadn't even put up a struggle. Because she'd wanted him. Wanted to know and be known completely. And how shameful was that?

Count Valieri, she thought, swallowing. That was how she must revert to thinking of him now. Her kidnapper—and not the glamorous and alluring lover whose hands and mouth had wrought such havoc with her senses only a little while ago.

She should have been warned when he'd told her he'd never taken a woman by force. Because, of course, he didn't have to.

I must have been his easiest conquest ever, she thought bitterly. His experience would tell him exactly how I was feeling. And he—he was unexpectedly kind.

But how could she ever face Jeremy again, knowing she'd committed the ultimate in betrayal by having a one night stand with his enemy?

But for Camillo, she would be in the Count's arms now, answering any and every passionate demand he might make of her. Oblivious to the nightmare of anguish and regret that would surely follow when she came back to her senses.

Except that it was her senses that had deceived

her in the first place, turning her into this un-recognisable creature—this *wanton* who'd shown Andrea Valieri a hunger she'd not known could exist—until that moment. And who'd sobbed and begged for a piercing, soaring satisfaction wholly outside her wildest dreams.

Just as he'd known it would be, because he had no illusions about her level of sexual sophistica-tion. Which was yet another humiliation to add to the growing list.

'Next time,' he'd said. Well, there would be no next time—just as there should have been no 'this time'. Because, she was back in control—of her mind as well as her body. And she would not allow herself to become his plaything again.

She heard the sound of voices, and shrank fur-ther under the sleeping bag. People talked about the cold light of day, she thought, and they were right. Because she was discovering that even bright sunlight had the power to make you shiver.

The curtain was pushed aside and Andrea came in, his face set.

'Camillo has brought you this,' he said, and placed her travel bag on the foot of the mattress.

She said slowly, staring at it. 'My things? Re-ally—my own things? You've given them back to me?'

A faint smile dispelled some of the grimness from his mouth. '*Sì, davvero.*' He paused, then added crisply, 'There is water heating for you to wash, but I would recommend that you make haste. Camillo tells me that the weather will change, bringing storms, and the road is already dangerous enough.'

She nodded. 'I—I'll be quick.'

'And I must pack this.' He bent and gathered up the sleeping bag into his arms leaving Maddie with no covering except the half-buttoned shirt. Which, suddenly, was not nearly enough.

With a swift nervous gesture, she huddled it around her as best she could, seeing the astonishment in his face turn to something more disturbing and much colder until, without a word, he turned on his heel and left her.

Maddie got up slowly from the mattress, aware she was shivering. She still ached from her fall, but the bruises were beginning to come out, and she could at least put her foot to the ground without hobbling.

The bag did not contain everything she'd brought to Italy, but it held a complete change of clothing, including underwear, and her toiletries, so she wasn't going to quibble. Even, she discovered, her watch had been returned. Her phrase book too,

but not, of course, her passport, wallet or tape recorder. That was too much to hope for.

But what, she wondered, as she made her swift
and rudimentary *toilette*, had brought about this
change of heart in her captor? Because that was
how she must regard him from now on. Keep all
the wrongs he'd done to her firmly in the forefront
of her mind.

And be thankful it had been no worse, she
thought, as she zipped up her black cut-offs and
pulled her flowered black and white tee shirt over
her head.

She had thought wearing her own clothes would
make her feel less vulnerable, but she was wrong
about that too. And knew that she would never
feel really safe until she was back in London. And
maybe not even then.

It took every scrap of courage she possessed to
walk out of the hut to where the jeep was waiting, but the two men were clearly more concerned
with the heavy cloud already gathering above the
mountain tops than her sensitivities.

She received a slight, formal inclination of the
head from Camillo, as he took her bag and opened
the rear door of the jeep for her. Andrea merely
sent her a brief, unsmiling glance with his curt,
'*Andiamo*. Let's go.'

She soon realised it was not a journey she would want to make twice in a lifetime.

Because the Count had not been exaggerating about the state of the road. In places, it was only just wide enough for the jeep, and deeply pot-holed with a serious drop on one side, which Maddie, sitting with her hands tightly clenched in her lap, wished she hadn't seen, especially when she heard the sound of stones and earth falling down into the valley as they passed.

She was sorely tempted to close her eyes, but that might have been interpreted as a sign of weakness, so she kept them open staring rigidly at the back of Andrea Valieri's dark head, only to remember with startling suddenness how thick and vibrant his hair had felt under her fingers.

Which was an equally dangerous road to take, she realised, when her body began to tingle with other memories. The awakening of fresh desires.

And better to be considered a coward than make an abject fool of herself all over again, she decided resolutely, leaning back and shutting her eyes tightly.

After a while, the jolting grew steadily less until, with a final lurch that brought her heart into her mouth, the jeep swung to the right and Maddie sat

up to discover they had emerged on to a reasonably decent road, descending between the hills.

'*Mai piu.* Never again.' The Count turned, giving
her a crooked smile. 'I shall arrange to have that
track closed *immediatamente.* Anyone wanting
Giacomo in future will have to reach him on foot.'

'How nice,' she said. 'To have that kind of power.'

The smile vanished. 'Especially when one can
use it to do good, Maddalena.' He paused. 'But
perhaps you have only encountered the other kind.'

And he turned away, addressing some quiet re-
mark to Camillo.

Which will teach me, Maddie thought, savaging
her lip once more, to try and score points.

She stared out of the window trying to concentrate on the spectacular scenery, striving to rebuild
the barriers in her mind and make them unassail-
able. To somehow recover some shreds of self-
respect and decency to take back to Casa Lupo.

Out of the corner of her eye, she saw a flash followed almost immediately by a low, threatening
rumble of thunder. At the same moment, the first
heavy drops of rain hit the windscreen. The threatened storm had arrived in all its malignant force.

Maddie caught her breath as she watched the
lightning forking down into the peaks as if it
planned to tear them apart. And the crash of the

thunder made it seem as if the mountains themselves had indeed succumbed to the eerie force and were beginning some lethal collapse, sweeping away everything in their path.

She'd never thought she'd be glad to see the house again, but, after nearly twenty minutes of driving, half-deafened, through the equivalent of a river, Casa Lupo's solid bulk seemed, absurdly, like a beacon of hope instead of a prison.

High iron gates swung open on to a short drive leading to the main entrance where Eustacio waited anxiously in the shelter of a huge black umbrella.

He rushed forward as the jeep halted, holding the umbrella over Maddie as he escorted her into the house, bombarding her with a stream of Italian which left her floundering.

'He is glad you are safe,' the Count supplied drily as he followed her into a massive hallway with a wide marble staircase at the far end.

'Oh,' said Maddie, forcing a smile. '*Grazie,* Eustacio.'

'He says too that Alfredo kisses your hands,' he added.

'Am I supposed to know who Alfredo is, or why he should want to do such a thing?' she inquired tautly.

'He is the father of Jolanda, now recovering at

home. In the eyes of her parents, you are a hero-ine, Maddalena.'

'Hardly that.' She flushed.

'Perhaps not,' he returned silkily. 'But let us leave them their illusions, *mia cara.*' He beckoned and a sheepish Luisa came forward, and took charge of Maddie's travel bag. 'She will escort you to your new accommodation.'

'Where this time? A dungeon?' She extended her wrists. 'Won't I need handcuffs?'

'A delicious thought which we might discuss in more detail later,' he said softly and unpardonably, and her flush deepened hectically.

'The only thing I wish to discuss with you, Count Valieri,' she said between her teeth, 'is the time of my flight back to London.'

And with all the dignity she could muster, she followed Luisa up the marble staircase, instinct telling her that he was watching her every step of the way. And warning her at the same time not to look back.

CHAPTER TEN

MADDIE FOLLOWED LUISA along the broad gallery, quivering with what she told herself was sheer temper, and nothing else.

Because he was not irresistible. That was what she had to keep telling herself. That was why she had to banish from her brain every one of those dangerous, intrusive memories, reminding her how his hands and mouth had swept her away to that endless moment of sweet, pulsating rapture.

She took a deep breath, clenching her hands in the pockets of her cut-offs. Yes, she'd behaved stupidly—in fact, unforgivably—earlier that day, but she was not about to disgrace herself a second time. And she had to stop beating herself up about it. Transfer her anger to him instead.

From now on, she told herself angrily, he could keep his questionable remarks, along with the smile in his eyes and its unspoken promise of future delight for the girl in Viareggio, or whatever other floozie might happen to take his fancy, as he seemed incapable of being faithful for even twenty-four hours.

And that was the end of it.

Her dungeon reference had not been serious, but after her escape, she'd expected to find herself shut up somewhere even more remote and twice as secure as the room with the doors had been.

Yet halfway along the gallery, Luisa had turned into a wide corridor and was briskly leading the way to a room at its end.

Maddie desperately tried to recall the Italian for 'Where are we going?' but without success. She really needed someone, she thought, to explain what was happening, even if it was in dodgy English with attitude.

'*Dov'e* Domenica?' she inquired. 'Is she still…?' She mimed someone throwing up.

Luisa shrugged and burst into a flood of incomprehensible speech, leaving Maddie none the wiser.

By this time they had reached the doors, and the girl flung them open and stood aside for Maddie to precede her into the room beyond.

She paused, catching her breath as she looked around her at a small but charming sitting room furnished with delicate sofas and chairs, all brocade-covered in blue, green and gold, grouped round a pretty marble fireplace, and a few elegant pieces of furniture including a writing desk at least two centuries old.

The walls were panelled in silk, and a cushioned seat ran the length of the long window.

I suppose this is more *trompe l'oeil*, and I'm really standing in a cupboard, Maddie thought, taking an uncertain step forward.

But the window, when she touched it, was the genuine article, looking down on to a formal garden, its geometric beds and gravelled paths now lit by a watery sun, making the stones and leaves sparkle.

She turned. 'It's lovely. *Bella.*'

Luisa beamed, then indicated the open door behind her.

Maddie walked past her into a large bedroom, occupied by a massive canopied bed curtained in dark blue silk. The headboard and posts were made from some rich golden-brown wood, intricately and beautifully carved with festoons of leaves, flowers and grapes.

The same wood had been used to build the row of fitted closets which framed another doorway. Beyond it, Maddie could see the gleam of ivory tiles, and the glimmer of gold fittings. A bathroom, she thought, with a sigh of longing. Warm water to wash the bits of dried leaf, dust and whatever insects had inhabited last night's mattress out of her hair, then to stretch out in and relax.

It felt like a wonderful dream. In fact, almost too wonderful…

She looked round at Luisa, who was placing the travel bag at the foot of the bed.

'For me?' She pointed to herself incredulously. 'I am to sleep—*dormire*—here?'

The girl nodded vigorously, her eyes dancing. She went to the closets and opened a couple of the doors, letting Maddie see that the rest of the clothes she'd brought to Italy were hanging there, or neatly folded in the adjoining drawers and shelves.

While in the next cupboard were the jewel-coloured nightgowns and robes which were all she'd had to wear up to now.

Side by side, Maddie thought, swallowing. These two different people that I've somehow become and their very different lives.

One of which had to go, and soon, because she was convinced that her enforced stay at the Casa Lupo had to be nearing its end, and that she would be returning home to sanity.

When Andrea Valieri would undoubtedly be hoping she would tell Jeremy and his father that she'd been treated well during her captivity.

Why else would she have been moved like this

from her former room to what had to be the best guest suite?

Although she had to admit that, apart from last night, for which she had only herself to blame, she'd been kept pretty much in the lap of luxury from the start. She'd even become quite fond of all those doors.

She swallowed. Whatever she said when she reached London, she would have to choose her words with great care. After all, the Sylvesters would also be looking for revenge.

And I wanted him punished, she reminded herself, feeling suddenly as if a knife was twisting slowly in her gut. I wanted them to lock him up and throw away the key—which could still happen. Only now, I'm not sure how I feel—or if even that is the truth...

'*Signorina*?'

She realised that Luisa was watching her anxiously and summoned a smile.

'*Grazie,* Luisa. I want nothing more.' She spread her hands. '*Niente.*'

The girl nodded, showed her the embroidered bell pull beside the fireplace in the sitting room, then whisked herself away.

Left alone, Maddie headed for the bathroom with her toiletries and a change of clothing.

While the vast tub was filling, she stripped, then slid into the gently steaming water, submerging herself completely. She sat up with a gasp, pushing back her drenched hair and wincing a little as she felt the sting of the heat on her grazes.

Most of the bruising had emerged too, making her look rather like a piebald pony, she thought ruefully. Not the ideal image for the long-awaited reunion with Jeremy. On the other hand, it was precisely because of the wait that she'd been forced into desperate action. And so she would tell him. Or would she…?

She found she was examining her body more carefully, as if searching for tell-tale fingerprints. A different mark of Cain left by Andrea Valieri to betray her. Or to remind her how close she had been to betraying herself.

But she wouldn't think like that, she told herself, reaching with determination for the shampoo. She couldn't afford to.

In the end, it took three washings and a lot of rinsing with the hand spray before her hair felt really clean again.

As for the rest of her, she thought, switching off the spray, then gathering her hair into a rope and wringing the water from it, well—that might be a different matter.

She heard a faint noise and turned her head.

Andrea Valieri was standing framed in the door-way, his expression arrested, intent as he watched her, his eyes glowing with inner fire.

He said softly, '*Che bella sirena,*' and took a step forward.

For a moment, Maddie was transfixed. When she found her voice, she said hoarsely, 'Don't come any closer.' She lifted her hands to cover her breasts, all too aware that she was being absurd, and hearing her tone become stormier in consequence. 'How dare you just—walk in here like this. Get out. Get out now.'

He halted, his brows lifting. '*Dio mio*—I am here to bring you this.' He held up the jar of antiseptic cream he'd used the previous evening. 'I thought that you might need it.'

She took a deep breath. 'Then kindly put it down and go.'

He complied with the first half of the request. 'Why so agitated, *carissima*?' he asked softly, as Maddie sat rigidly, hands still clamped to her chest. 'Your body is hardly a mystery to me.'

'I don't need any reminder of that,' she said, adding bitterly, 'To my abiding shame.'

'Ah.' Andrea was silent for a moment, then gave

her a level look. 'For my part, I remember only de-light. But you had only to say "No", Maddalena.'

'I'm aware of that.' She bit her lip. 'Do you imag-ine it improves the situation?'

'At this moment, I doubt that anything could,' he returned with faint dryness. 'So, why did you not stop me when you had the chance?'

'Because I'd had a terrible time in your beastly forest,' she flung back at him. 'And seeing that wolf was the final straw. I was scared—stressed out and you—you took advantage of me.'

'Why, Maddalena, what a little hypocrite you are,' he said softly. 'If we had not been interrupted, any advantage would have been mutual, and you know that, so do not pretend.'

'I wasn't thinking straight. I didn't know what I was doing,' Maddie defended a mite feebly. She rallied. 'Unlike you, *signore.* You, of course, had your own agenda.'

He shrugged. 'I wanted to make love to you, *mia bella.* It is hardly a state secret.'

'Is a few hours of celibacy really such a strain?' she asked witheringly. 'You'd only just got back from your lady in Viareggio when you came after me.'

'Portofino,' he corrected evenly. 'I was visiting a lady in Portofino not Viareggio.'

Maddie gasped. 'You think the location actually makes some difference?'

'When making accusations, I find it is better to be factually accurate.' He paused. 'I have noticed that you do not seem to share my view.'

'I have no wish to share anything with you, Count Valieri,' she said stormily. 'And that includes this roof. When will I be free to leave here?'

'I regret that the decision still remains in other hands than mine, *mia bella.* Or is that something else you prefer to forget?' He reached down the white towelling bathrobe hanging on the back of the door, and held it out to her. 'That water must be getting cold, Maddalena, and I would not wish you to take a chill.'

He absorbed her mutinous expression, sighed, then, draping the robe over the side of the tub, he turned his back and walked to the door.

Maddie could not pretend to be sorry as she scrambled out of the tepid depths of the bath, and huddled herself into the robe. It dwarfed her, reaching to her ankles, and the sash went twice round her slim waist before being tied in a secure knot.

As she rolled up the sleeves, a disturbing thought struck her. She said, 'Is this robe yours?'

'*Sì.*' He turned. 'But it has been laundered, so you will escape contamination.'

She remembered other things—like that handsomely carved bed in the other room, and her mouth dried. She gestured round her. 'And this bathroom—these other rooms are yours too?'

'*Naturalmente*.' He leaned casually against the doorframe. 'The whole house belongs to me, so how could it be otherwise?'

She said, 'That—isn't what I mean, and you know it.'

'No,' he said. 'You are concerned that you are sharing my private suite.'

'Not concerned,' she said. 'Furious. Are you surprised?'

'I think there is little more you could do to surprise me, Maddalena. So, let us rather say—disappointed.'

'Why?' Maddie lifted her chin. 'Because your nasty little scheme isn't going to work?'

The dark brows lifted. 'Is that how you regard my wish to be your lover?'

'Now who's being a hypocrite?' she demanded stonily.

'My desire for you is real and genuine, Maddalena.' He smiled suddenly, and she felt her heart thud. He added softly, 'Let me join you for the siesta later and I will prove it.'

'And that's really the only thing on your mind,

Count Valieri?' Fighting the sweet seductive wave of warmth his words had induced, Maddie shook her head. 'I don't believe it.'

'With you in my arms, *carissima,* how could it be possible for me to think of anything else?' He paused. 'And it might be that I also wish to keep you close to me to avoid any further unwise attempts at escape.'

'Or you might also be looking for another way to punish the Sylvesters,' she said. 'Or at least Jeremy. Which seems far more likely.'

'Why—when I have done what is necessary already?'

'Because they haven't responded to your blackmail.' She drew a painful breath. 'So taking me, and letting my fiancé know about it, would be a very special form of revenge. The stiletto through the ribs, up to its hilt.'

In the silence that followed, Andrea was no longer smiling. 'What a vivid imagination you have, *mia bella,*' he drawled. 'So what do you think I would say to him? That you indeed have hair like the sun, but your body is sheer moonlight. That you have a tiny mole on your right hip that I have kissed. That you taste of honey and roses. All the exquisite intimate details about you that he must already know and which would hurt him the most to hear from another man?'

'Yes.' Maddie felt as if she was burning all over. 'If—if that's how you wish to put it.'

'I do not.' The words hung harshly in the air. 'I take the reparation owing to me and no more. What you suggest is an insult—to yourself, Maddalena, as well as to me.'

'Then let me go back to that other room.' *Away from here. From you.* She added with difficulty, 'Please...'

'But it does not please me,' he said curtly. 'You will stay here, but only as a matter of security. You will sleep alone. I shall use the bedroom that adjoins yours.'

She lifted her chin. 'Does the door between us have a lock?'

'*Sì.*' He paused, his mouth twisting. 'But no key.'

'And I'm expected to believe you—trust you?' she asked raggedly. 'Not a chance, *signore.* But I promise you this. That if you dare to come near me again I'll fight you. And next time it will be with every breath in my body.'

'How quickly things can change,' he drawled cynically. 'But your vow will never be fulfilled, Maddalena. Because in this next time you speak of, my moonlight girl, you will come to me, of your own free will and giving yourself completely. And that, too, is a promise.'

He walked out, closing the door behind him, leaving her to stare after him, a hand pressed to her throat.

It soon became a very long day.

Maddie began it sitting on the edge of the bath, waiting for her inner trembling to subside. Or for Andrea to return...

When it became apparent this would not happen, she rose slowly to her feet, took the hand-dryer from the wall and carefully attended to her hair, smoothing it into shining order once more.

Hair like the sun...

Her heart pounded as she remembered the other things he'd said. Not that they bore any real relation to herself. They were simply the well-worn phrases of a practised womaniser, and she should treat them with the contempt they deserved.

His parting shot would have been unforgivable if it had not been so ludicrous. As if she would ever offer herself in that way. So why had it reduced her to stunned silence? she asked herself shivering.

But it was his query 'Why did you not stop me?' that she found beating in her brain, because pleading 'temporary insanity' was no excuse at all, and she knew it.

At the same time it occurred to her that if Jeremy had ever thought her body was like moonlight, he hadn't mentioned it.

She applied the antiseptic cream Andrea had brought her, then, leaving the borrowed robe in a crumpled heap on the tiled floor, she dressed in a plain blue skirt, and short-sleeved white top, and made her way back to the sitting room, curling up on the window seat.

Honey and roses.

She closed her eyes, emptying her mind, forcing away, with the words, memories of the magic of his lips and hands. Trying to restore herself to the rational world, but without success.

It was almost a relief when a tap on the door signalled the arrival of Eustacio with her lunch—soup and a baked pasta dish in a delicious sauce, followed by fresh fruit. After making sure she had everything she needed, he informed her in his stilted English that his Excellency the Count had been called away on urgent business, but hoped she would do him the honour of dining with him that evening.

She could produce all kinds of feasible and dignified excuses to make it quite clear to her host that she didn't wish to be alone with him under any circumstances. For heaven's sake, the list had to be endless, with self-preservation at the top.

Instead she found herself murmuring her acquiescence.

And as she ate her meal, she wondered where the urgent business had taken him. Viareggio— or Portofino?

Not that it was any of her concern. What mattered were his negotiations with the Sylvesters, because surely this situation couldn't go on much longer.

Please, she whispered under her breath. Please let it be so. Because I have to get out of here. I must…

As afternoon passed into evening, she changed into the black dress she'd worn at the opera, and was back, sitting on the window seat, looking down into the darkening garden when Luisa came to fetch her.

She followed the girl back down to the hall and watched as she pressed a section of panelling which immediately swung inwards.

Easy when you know how, she thought, bracing herself as she walked into the *salone* beyond. And stopped, staring at the empty space above the fireplace.

For a moment, she thought she was being subjected to yet another trick of the eye. That if she blinked, or moved slightly to left or right, the picture that usually hung there would be in its accustomed place.

But as she moved closer, she realised all that remained was a slight discoloration on the surrounding wall.

'I had it removed.'

Maddie swung round and saw Andrea standing in the doorway. Unsmiling, he was wearing an elegant dark suit, and, apart from his loosened tie and the open top button on his shirt, looked remote and powerful as if he was about to chair some vital board meeting.

There was certainly no trace of the lover who had shown her a glimpse of Paradise that morning. But that had to be a good thing...

She experienced a sensation like a fist slowly clenching in her stomach, and hurried into speech.

'Removed? But why?'

He shrugged. 'After your encounter with a live wolf in the village last night, it seemed wiser. A reminder of the experience might cause you more fright—more stress,' he added pointedly. 'And neither of us would wish that.'

Maddie flushed, struggling to keep her voice

steady. 'But the protection of the species—all the work that's been done—is part of your heritage.'

'To Count Guillermo, the cause was admirable,' he said. 'However its purpose has been achieved, and my own interests lie in other directions. Please believe that the absence of the picture is no hardship. I would prefer this place to become again what it was intended to be—the House of Summer.' He gave a faint smile. 'You have provided the incentive.'

'The House of Summer,' she repeated slowly. 'That sounds—really lovely.'

'I shall make it so.'

In the pause which followed, Andrea's eyes met hers and the silence between them suddenly began to change. To shimmer with tension, and an awareness as endless as the space between them.

So why did it seem that just one small step would take her into his arms? As if some unseen, unknown magnetic force was drawing her to him.

Drawing her to her own destruction...

A realisation that gave her the strength to act. To break the spell that held her before it was too late.

She moved, swiftly and restlessly, tearing her gaze from his and staring down at the floor as she wrapped her arms round her body in a gesture of total negation. And heard across the room the harshness of the brief sigh that escaped him.

A sigh that found an echo in the depths of her being, but was not uttered aloud.

Instead she heard herself say with quiet intensity, 'Let me go. You have to let me go. You boasted once that you'd never taken a woman by force, yet that's how you're keeping me here. It can't go on like this, and you know it.'

'I do indeed know,' he said. 'But it will not continue for much longer.'

Her throat constricted painfully. She made herself look up. Look at him. 'You mean there's news? You've heard from London?'

'No,' he said. 'I have not.'

'Then end it,' she said passionately. 'Cut your losses and send me back. Because he—Jeremy's father—will never give in. You don't know what you're up against.'

'You are wrong, Maddalena. I have known for a long time. Almost my whole life. And I too do not—give in.' He paused. 'And you? Are you still determined to marry into this family?'

She lifted her chin. 'I'm marrying the man I love. Not his family. A very different proposition.'

His mouth curled. 'I am glad you think so. I hope you will not be disappointed.' He walked to the drinks trolley, and mixed her a Campari soda, pouring whisky for himself.

He handed her the drink, and Maddie took it, being careful to avoid brushing his fingers with hers.

He raised his glass, his mouth twisting. 'To your future happiness, *carissima*.' He added sardonically, 'Whatever form it takes.'

He swallowed half the whisky, and turned away.

'To happiness,' Maddie echoed huskily, and found the pungent taste of the Campari turning sour in her throat as she drank.

CHAPTER ELEVEN

DINNER WAS AN awkward meal, interspersed with silences that neither of them seemed to wish or be able to break.

But when, at the end of the meal, Eustacio, following a signal from his master, brought a bottle of grappa to the table and placed it beside him, Maddie hastily finished her coffee and excused herself.

And tried to ignore the soft taunt, 'Running away, *mia bella?*' which followed her as Eustacio conducted her to the hidden door and back to her room.

The bed had been turned down, on one side only, she saw with relief, while her own lawn nightdress had been fanned out across the coverlet.

But she still felt uneasy about the unlockable door which was all that separated them, especially if it was Andrea's intention to drink himself to extinction on that potent Italian spirit before coming to his room.

Her brave words about fighting him off might

just come back to haunt her, she thought, biting her lip.

But her rest was untroubled, and the next time she opened her eyes, she found sunshine filling the room and the ever-smiling Luisa bringing her a breakfast tray.

On which was a note in a familiar hand.

She fortified herself with coffee and hot rolls spread with honey before opening it.

'Forgive me for last night,' it began abruptly. 'I spoke churlishly. But this is a new and beautiful day and I shall be driving to the coast later this morning. I hope that you allow me to make amends by agreeing to be my companion, and joining me downstairs at eleven o clock.' It was signed with his initials.

Maddie read it twice, her brows creased. Was 'I shall be driving' to be taken literally, or would Camillo once again be behind the wheel?

Common sense told her that to spend a whole day in Andrea's sole company would be playing with fire.

On the other hand, refusing his invitation was tantamount to admitting as much. Telling him she was scared of being alone with him.

And not because she feared he might break his word and try to make love to her, she thought unhappily. On the contrary, it was because she couldn't trust herself.

Something that, for her own piece of mind, she couldn't allow him to suspect. Ever...

So when Eustacio came for the tray, she handed back the note saying quietly, 'Please thank Count Valieri and tell him I shall look forward to it.'

He repeated the words carefully, bowed slightly and left.

Leaving Maddie to review her limited wardrobe.

In the end she chose a plain white linen skirt teamed with a black tunic-style top, fastening her hair at the nape of her neck with a silver clip.

Neat and businesslike rather than seductive, she reassured herself as Luisa conducted her downstairs to meet him.

Andrea, in cream chinos and a dark red polo shirt, was standing in the hall, clearly issuing some last-minute instructions to Eustacio, but he broke off at Maddie's approach, looking up at her, the smile in his eyes jolting her like a sudden electrical charge.

For a second she hesitated, telling herself it was not too late to change her mind and scurry back to her room for a dull but safe day reading.

Except that this was probably her only chance to see something of Italy. She could not imagine

Jeremy permitting her to return any time soon, if ever.

So, she completed her sedate descent, just as if her heart was not hammering fit to break out of her ribcage, and walked across the tiled expanse of the entrance hall to join him.

She said, 'Isn't this rather a risk?'

His brows lifted. 'In what way?'

'By inviting me to go with you, back into the real world.' Maddie swallowed. 'Aren't you afraid I'll run away again?'

He gave a faint shrug. 'There is certainly that possibility. But will you?'

They looked at each other, Andrea's gaze intense, questioning as it locked with hers.

And she heard herself say, 'No.'

He gave a slight nod. 'Then let us go.'

It was a car she had never seen before, a sleek open-topped sports model, instantly confirming that Camillo would not be with them, either as driver or chaperon.

Maddie settled herself into the passenger seat, tying a scarf over her hair and hoping she looked more composed than she felt as the engine purred into life like a waking lion.

They took the road that snaked down into the valley. She found that he drove well, if rather faster than she was used to, but this was, after all, a familiar road with only local traffic, and very little of that.

She said, 'I'm glad the storms have gone.'

'They will return.' He shrugged a shoulder. 'But not too soon, I hope.'

'Or at least until I've gone home.' She kept her tone light but positive. Making it clear that was her real focus. Her main concern.

'*Naturalmente.*' Andrea's voice was silky. 'Yet who knows when that will be?'

'And how my life will be when I get there.' She spoke half to herself as all the doubts and fears of her first days at Casa Lupo suddenly returned. As she pictured Nigel Sylvester's fury at having to pay to rescue her, and felt cold inside.

'What do you mean?' He was frowning.

Maddie bit her lip, vexed at that involuntary moment of self-revelation. 'For one thing—will I have a job to go back to? I vanish off the face of the earth for days on end and come back empty-handed. That's hardly a good career move.'

'But you are going to be married,' he said. 'Therefore such considerations can hardly matter.'

She gasped. 'I can't believe you just said that—that blatant piece of male chauvinism. You should be ashamed.'

'But I was just echoing a familiar viewpoint, *certamente*,' he said softly. 'Or are you going to tell me that your *fidanzato* approves of your becoming a working wife? Because I warn you, Maddalena, I shall not believe you.'

She turned her head sharply, staring at him. When she could control her voice, she said, 'Is there anything about me that you don't know?'

'*Sì*,' he said. A smile touched the corners of his mouth. 'One last secret that I have yet to make mine. As you are already aware, *mia bella*, so let us not pretend.'

'At least,' she said huskily, 'there is something that I can keep from you.'

'*Forse sì, forse no.* I would say, *carissima*, it is all in the lap of the gods. And I can still hope.' He paused. '*Tuttavia*, there is so much you could learn about me, so much I wish to tell you, yet you never ask.'

She clasped her hands tightly in her lap to conceal the fact that they were trembling. 'I would prefer to change the subject.'

'*Certamente.* What would you like to discuss?'

'You said—the coast.' Geography should be safe enough. 'But I know very little about this area,' she went on brightly. 'So, where exactly are you taking me?'

'Oh, did I not say?' He shot her an amused glance. 'I have business in Portofino.' He added, mockingly, 'Private business.'

There was silence. Maddie sat staring straight ahead of her, rigid with temper and disbelief.

What in hell was he trying to prove? That the women in his life were so amenable they didn't mind sharing his favours turn and turn about?

And was that what he'd had planned for her too—if she'd committed the ultimate folly and become his lover?

Well, she thought, her throat tightening, at least she'd been spared that particular humiliation. But being forced to meet his current mistress was quite another story. And cruel to them both.

A sharp unfamiliar pain was twisting slowly inside her, tying her into trembling knots. At the same time, she was aware of an almost uncontrollable desire to scream, hit him, and burst into tears.

My God, she thought incredulously. I'm jealous. For the first time in my life, I'm jealous. This is how it feels, and I hate it. I hate myself. After all, it isn't as if—as if…

And closed her mind as the inner pain deepened, intensified.

One day she would be leaving all this behind,

forgetting it as if it was a bad dream. That's what she had to believe. To cling to.

And if it taught her to value the happiness waiting for her even more, well—that was all to the good too.

Just the same, she would have given anything to be able to order him to turn the car round and take her back to the house, but she knew any such request would be laughed at then ignored.

So, she dug her nails into the palms of her hands and prepared to endure.

It was a quiet journey.

Apart from asking once or twice if she was comfortable, Andrea said nothing, and it occurred to Maddie, as she replied politely and briefly in the affirmative, that he too might be having second thoughts about the wisdom of this trip.

At first, she'd been able to concentrate fiercely on the spectacular scenery. When they eventually joined the major road, there was little to absorb her but the busy and fast-moving traffic. And it wasn't enough.

Her anger had subsided, leaving a deep, aching hollow in its place, with tears never too far away. She could feel them pricking at her eyes, and burning in her throat, but she wouldn't allow as much as one drop to fall.

At the same time, she knew she had no right to feel so wretched—so desolate, and she was disturbed by the intensity of her own emotions, and reluctant to contemplate what this might signify.

Knowing only this trip was a mistake, and she wanted it to be over.

Portofino occupied the edge of a small peninsula, and the road leading to it was narrow and twisted like a snake.

Just as if she wasn't nervous enough already, thought Maddie.

'There is no need for concern.' He must have noticed the tense clasping of her hands in her lap. 'I know this road well.'

'I'm sure you do.' She instantly regretted the slight snap in her tone, adding with cool if inaccurate civility, 'And I'm not at all worried.'

'*Certo che no*!' he returned. 'Of course not.' He paused. 'Cars are not allowed into the village, so we will have to park and walk a little way.'

'A walk would suit me very well,' she said. 'A long one, perhaps, while you transact your private business.'

'Ah,' he said softly. 'But for that, *mia bella,* I need you at my side. Did I not make that clear?'

She gave him a bitter look. 'Yes,' she said. 'But I hoped for everyone's sake that you might have changed your mind.'

'But mine is not the mind that needs to change, Maddalena.' There was an oddly harsh note in his voice. 'As I intend to prove to you very soon.'

He turned the wheel and swung the car into a small crowded parking area overlooking the bay, slotting it expertly between two four-wheel drives. He walked round to the passenger side and opened the door for her to alight, extending a helping hand which she ignored.

She stood for a moment, straightening the creases in her skirt, and smoothing her hair, released from the scarf, with unsteady fingers.

'*Andiamo.*' Andrea's hand was firm on her arm.

She tried to hang back. 'Please—I can't do this. I'm not ready...'

'Ready or not, it is time you knew the truth. Learned why you were brought here.' He paused. 'And some of the reasons why I have not let you go.'

They set off down the steep hill, but turned off after a couple of hundred yards on to a lane, little more than a track.

'Where are we going?'

'To pay a visit to the Villa Gabriele.'

She said hoarsely, 'Do you realise how cruel you're being—to her?' Almost adding, 'And to me,' but stopping herself just in time.

'This is not cruelty,' he said. 'But necessity.'

They rounded a bend, and the house was in front of them, honey-coloured in the sunshine behind its wrought iron gates. Large, too, and surrounded by flower gardens, and with charming balconies to its upper floor windows.

No expense spared, thought Maddie, a fist clenching in her chest. And is this trip designed to show me what I'm missing by turning him down as a lover? Is there another villa, somewhere, waiting for a mistress? The new name on the list?

Andrea took her up the path, and the short flight of steps to the front door, where he rang the bell.

Almost before Maddie could draw breath, the door opened and she found herself confronted by Domenica. She greeted Andrea with a bob of her head and a polite murmur, but for the astonished Maddie there was just the usual unfriendly glance.

What on earth is she doing here? Maddie asked herself as they walked through an airy hall into a large *salone* at the rear of the house, and out on to a terrace overlooking Portofino and the sea.

A woman dressed in black was standing by the stone balustrade, and she turned quickly. But this was not the sexy blonde or the voluptuous brunette of Maddie's imagination.

This woman was older, her dark hair, drawn back into a heavy chignon, streaked with silver. Her face was still beautiful because of its exquisite bone structure but at the same time it was strained, even haggard, her wide amber eyes fixed on Maddie with the same inimical expression used by Domenica.

She turned towards Andrea speaking rapidly in Italian, the sun creating sparks of fire from the diamonds on her slender hands as she gestured angrily.

He said gently, 'Mammina, it had to be. You know this. Now speak English or Maddalena will not be able to understand.' He looked down at Maddie standing like a statue beside him. '*Carissima,* I wish you to meet…'

'But I know who it is,' she said hoarsely. 'It's Floria Bartrando. The missing opera singer I came to Italy to interview. I—I can't believe it.'

'She is also my mother,' he said. 'The Contessa Valieri.'

Maddie felt as if she'd been winded. 'How—how do you do,' she managed.

But her greeting was not returned, and the Contessa did not offer a hand to be shaken.

'I had no intention of ever speaking to you, *signorina*.' It was a rich, lovely voice still, in spite of its overt hostility. 'We meet now only at my son's insistence. I do not willingly receive a young woman who openly allies herself with my enemies.'

Maddie's stunned astonishment was fading fast to be replaced by indignation as she registered the contempt in the older woman's tone.

'Enemies?' she repeated. 'What do you mean? If you're talking about my fiancé and his father, they knew exactly why I was coming here, and it was obvious they'd never heard of you.'

Yet, at the same time, hadn't Jeremy told her that his father was violently opposed to the idea of her visiting Italy...

'No,' said the Contessa icily. 'Andrea's father took great care that they should not do so. He knew trouble was coming and he was afraid of how it might end, so he insisted our secret must wait for better times in order to protect me. To protect my reputation. My career.'

'I don't understand any of this,' Maddie protested. 'What trouble?'

'Perhaps it would be better to start at the beginning,' Andrea suggested quietly. 'This is a time for explanation, not to create further misunderstandings.' He took his mother's hand and kissed it. 'Mammina, please try to accept that Maddalena is innocent of all blame in this affair.'

'All blame?' The Contessa pursed her lips. 'I wonder. But let us deal with the matter, *figlio mio*, as you suggest.'

She waved to a table and chairs set under a striped awning. 'Shall we be seated?'

Maddie hesitated. She didn't want to be here, she realised. She didn't want to hear what they might be going to say. She felt suddenly scared, as if she was standing at a door which might lead to a bottomless abyss, where only one unwary step could lead to her destruction.

Turn back, an inner voice was prompting her. You don't have to hear these things. You're the innocent party in all this, as he's just said. So, refuse to listen and turn back to safety.

Yet in her heart, she knew she had forfeited safety from the moment she'd decided to research the story of a lost soprano. From that moment on, she'd simply been a puppet, manipulated by forces she had never encountered before like hatred and revenge.

And, if she was to be wholly honest, haunted— torn apart by a sexual desire that was also totally outside her experience.

I have to know, she thought, a faint shiver running through her in spite of the sun's warmth. I can't spend the rest of my life wondering why this happened to me.

When they were seated, Domenica appeared carrying a tray with glasses and a tall jug of fresh lemonade, clanking with ice cubes.

She's like a different person, Maddie thought, observing the warm smile that transformed the other's features when she spoke to the Contessa. But not with me, she added ruefully, finding herself once more on the receiving end of another surly glare as Domenica retreated indoors.

Accepting the lemonade Andrea had poured for her, she said, 'I'm ready to listen.'

He was silent for a moment. 'I must begin with a question,' he said at last. 'During your time with the Sylvesters, have you ever heard the name Marchetti?'

Maddie frowned. 'Yes—once. Jeremy was saying that Sylvesters used to have foreign directors on the board. I'm sure that was one of the names.'

He nodded unsmilingly. 'It was. The last to serve was Benito Marchetti, but his poor health did not allow him to play an active part. That role was taken by his son Tommaso. He had spent much of his boyhood in England, and had even been to school with Nigel Sylvester, with whom he had become friends. Great things were expected of him. Accordingly, when he was told there were problems with the branch in Milano, he decided to investigate personally.'

He paused again. 'While he was there, he met a girl, a young soprano who was also making a name for herself, and who had come to the city for some specialised coaching by a Maestro Benzano before returning to Rome to sing the role of Gilda in "Rigoletto".

'We fell in love,' said Floria Valieri. The harshness had gone. Her gaze was remote, tender. 'It should not have happened. It was madness. We were too young, just starting our careers. Yet suddenly nothing mattered but each other. We were overwhelmed by our feelings, our need for each other.

She shook her head. 'I had never realised that sometimes it can be like that. That in a moment two lives can change forever.'

She smiled faintly. 'We told no-one, but Tommaso's great friend who had introduced us guessed somehow, and promised to keep our secret. He did so his whole life long.'

Maddie's voice was barely more than a whisper. 'You mean—Count Valieri?'

'*Sì.*' Andrea took up the story. 'They decided that when her season in Rome was over, they would be married. But Tommaso returned to London in order to make enquiries into some of the things he had learned in Milano.'

'What kind of things?' Maddie's heart was beating an alarm.

'Sums of money,' he said. 'Lost in a labyrinth of transactions that led nowhere. Currency deals that could not be traced. Other apparent irregularities. All the evidence suggested that one person was responsible, but Tommaso could not—did not want to believe it.'

He sighed. 'He told Cesare Valieri, who warned him to be careful. But it was too late. Soon after his return to London he himself was arrested and charged with embezzlement. All those strange elusive deals he had discovered were suddenly being traced back to him.'

'How much was he supposed to have stolen?' Maddie's mouth was dry.

He shrugged. 'In the region of half a million pounds. At his first hearing, bail was refused and he had to await trial in prison. While he was there, he wrote a letter to his *fidanzata*, telling her that he had been framed and promising he would prove his innocence very soon. He told her that she must not go to England or become involved in any way, that she must continue with "Rigoletto" and write to him only through his lawyer.

'He also wrote to Cesare, imposing the same sanctions and begging him to take care of his beloved, if the worst happened.

'He told them both that he had no doubt that the case against him would be dismissed and the real embezzler brought to justice. He also told them the culprit's name.'

Maddie stared at the Contessa. She said thickly, 'I know what you're going to say, and I can't—I won't believe it.'

'Nor did Tommaso—at first.' The Contessa sipped some lemonade. 'The man had been his friend. It seemed impossible that he should steal and lay a trail to a false bank account so my Tommaso would be blamed. *Tuttavia,* it was the truth.'

She looked back at Maddie, her gaze unwavering. 'Understand this, *signorina.* Nigel Sylvester is a criminal. A thief—and, in the eyes of God, a murderer too.'

CHAPTER TWELVE

'No.' MADDIE WAS on her feet, her glass overturned and the remains of her lemonade dripping on to the flagstones of the terrace. 'No, that I will never believe. Not even he…' She stopped with a gasp as she realised what she was saying.

'I said a murderer in the eyes of God.' The Contessa's tone was austere. 'No, he did not do the deed himself or hire someone for the purpose. I acquit him of that. But it was Nigel Sylvester's plotting to cover his own crime that caused my Tommaso to be in jail, and in that way he was responsible for his death.'

'There was a fight in the prison,' Andrea explained bleakly. 'Two men attacking someone smaller—weaker. Tommaso went to the victim's aid, but one of the assailants had a piece of sharpened metal, and, in the struggle, my father was stabbed in the throat, it seems accidentally. He bled to death before help could come.'

'Your father?' Maddie asked hoarsely. 'You're saying *he* was your father? But I thought...'

The Contessa lifted a hand. She said heavily, 'I had told Tommaso that I was to have his child before he went back to London. And I was glad I had done so, telling myself I had given him a reason to fight to prove his innocence. As he would have done, if he had lived,' she added, pressing a lace-edged handkerchief to her lips. 'But the case died with him, leaving this unjust—this unforgivable stain on his name—his character.'

Maddie sank back on her chair, her legs trembling.

She said, 'But what can you do?'

The Contessa's eyes flashed. 'I can make Nigel Sylvester pay for what he did. A poet once wrote that the mills of God grind slowly, and that one has only to wait in patience for vengeance to be accomplished.'

'But you can't actually prove anything,' Maddie argued. *The man's going to be my father-in-law, for God's sake. I have to defend him.* 'Besides Signor Marchetti might have been mistaken and blamed the wrong man. It's quite possible.'

She took a deep breath. 'You loved him. You want to believe the best of him, and I understand that. But his innocence doesn't necessarily make Nigel Sylvester guilty.'

'But there is proof,' said the Contessa. 'Tommaso wrote down every detail of his investigation, and hid the papers under the floorboards in his London apartment.'

'He told only Cesare what he had done,' Andrea said quietly. 'And his friend found the files while he was settling my father's affairs, even though the flat had been searched by the police and later ransacked again—by someone else.'

Maddie swallowed. 'But if the Count had this evidence, why didn't he use it then and there?'

'Because the case was officially closed. And also he knew that my father had not trusted the policeman leading the investigation. He feared the files might simply—vanish.'

'But above all he was thinking of me,' said the Contessa. 'Because when I heard the news, I was suddenly in this dark place where I could not think—where I could barely speak. I could certainly not sing. Not then. Not since. For a while, I even thought I would lose my baby.'

Maddie felt the breath catch in her throat.

Involuntarily, her eyes turned to Andrea—to the cool, proud face, its austerity contradicted by the golden glow of his eyes. The firm mouth that could curve into a smile to wrench at her heart, and bring her to the edge of surrender with its beguiling warmth. The potent sensual promise of the lean, muscular body, once so briefly yet unforgettably close to hers.

A cold hand seemed to touch her, turning her blood to ice as she thought, 'You might never have been born. I might never have seen you. Never been held in your arms. And I can't bear to think about it. I can't...'

'Cesare had been asked to protect me,' the older woman continued. 'A promise he took most seriously. He felt that I needed peace and a safe sanctuary in which to recover, to regain my strength and my sanity. And somehow find acceptance.'

Her sudden smile was unexpectedly tender. 'All these things he gave me and more. Finally, he offered his name to me and to the child I was expecting, asking for nothing in return. We were married in secret at a church in the hills above Trimontano and went back to live at Casa Lupo, where Andrea was born and raised as Cesare's own child.'

'But surely people must have been looking for you,' Maddie protested. 'You were already famous and you just—disappeared.'

The Contessa shrugged. 'But no-one knew where to look.' She added coolly, 'You would not have done so either, *signorina*, had you not been led here.'

Maddie bit her lip. 'I need no reminder of that.' She paused. 'But you had the most beautiful voice. How could you bear to give up singing?'

'For a long while, I felt as if I was drowning in my unhappiness. But as time passed, and my son was born, my life changed for the better. I became a wife to the husband who loved me and in this new contentment, my voice began to return a little.

'But I made a solemn vow that I would never sing publicly again until Nigel Sylvester had paid for what he did. Nor will I, although I am now hoping my return in concert will not be too long delayed.'

'Which was how you tempted me.' Maddie sighed. 'What would you have done if the company had sent someone else?'

'It was not our only plan. We would simply have begun again.' The Contessa gave her a thin smile. 'Perhaps in the Maldives.'

Maddie drew a shaken breath. 'You actually knew where I'd be going on honeymoon?'

'The Sylvester family has no secrets from us,' the Contessa informed her calmly. 'My late husband decided to have them watched, and over the past few years the surveillance has intensified.'

Maddie bent her head. 'I see.'

'There was no personal enmity towards you,' said Floria Valieri. 'But we felt you could be useful. As it has proved.' She paused. 'If not altogether wise.'

'I can promise you that,' Maddie said coldly.

'You can certainly hope.' The Contessa shrugged again. *Tuttavia,* it was the information that Nigel Sylvester was to become a member of your House of Lords that gave us the opportunity to take from him the very thing he has worked and schemed for. The supreme accolade for his life's work. A career founded on greed, betrayal and deceit.' She almost spat the words.

'And you really think he will let that go?' Maddie asked incredulously. She shook her head. 'Never in this world.'

'He has no choice.' Andrea spoke. 'Among my father's papers is a letter in the man Sylvester's own hand, begging him for the sake of their past friendship and the bank's good name not to continue with his exposure of the fraud, and offering to put matters right. He must have assumed it would never be found.'

'But if you have this evidence, why did you need me?' Maddie spread her hands. 'It makes no sense.'

'Because we require more from him.' Andrea's

tone hardened. 'He must write another letter to us admitting his guilt, not just for the fraud, but for the betrayal which led to my father's death.' He paused. 'In addition, he must refuse the life peerage that has been offered to him.'

Maddie looked away. She said bleakly, 'Then I'm not surprised he hasn't replied. You—you're really asking for your pound of flesh.'

The Contessa's brows lifted. 'I would call it natural justice, *signorina*. You blame us for this?'

'No,' Maddie said dully. 'In the circumstances, I don't think I can.' She swallowed. 'But maybe you can also understand that I wish I'd never heard of you.'

She rose and walked over to the balustrade, its stone warm under her hands as she looked down at the view—the tumble of houses among the vivid green of cypresses, cedars and palm trees leading down to Portofino's horseshoe harbour lined with buildings in yellow, ochre and cream, and, beyond that, the restless azure glitter of the sea.

She wondered how anything could be so beautiful, so brilliant, when everything in the safe world she had longed to return to had become so dark and so ugly.

Be careful what you wish for, she thought, because it might come true. Isn't that the old saying? Maybe I should have remembered that.

And it occurred to her that a simple ransom demand would have been far easier to bear.

And thought, I don't know what to do...

Behind her she heard a murmur of voices, and then the receding click of high heels across the flagstones, signalling that Floria Valieri had returned to the house.

Andrea came to stand beside her. 'Forgive me, Maddalena.' His voice was gentle. 'But it was time you heard the truth.'

She went on staring down at a vista that had become strangely blurred.

'Jeremy knows nothing about all this,' she said, her voice trembling. 'Nothing, I tell you.'

'*Naturalmente.*' His tone was wry.

She turned on him. 'You don't believe that?'

'It is what you believe,' he said. 'That is enough.'

There was a note in his voice that troubled her, making her heartbeat quicken.

Swiftly, she changed the subject. 'So Domenica really works for your mother. Well that explains the hostility. And now I've met the Contessa, I can understand the devotion too.'

She bit her lip. 'I wish I could have known her under different circumstances.'

'A desire that I share.'

Heartbeat still hammering, Maddie hurried on. 'And I'm glad she found happiness with your—stepfather.'

He inclined his head gravely. 'He was the best of men.' He paused. 'He loved her from the first, but when she met Tommaso, one look was enough to tell him he had lost her. He told himself then that a better man had won.'

Maddie stared at the horizon. 'Perhaps he should have spoken up anyway,' she said. 'Not been so noble.'

'But how can we truly judge at this distance?'

'Isn't that exactly what you're doing now?' she asked stonily, and turned towards the house. 'May we leave, please.'

'Not yet,' he said. 'We are to have lunch with my mother.'

'I couldn't eat.'

'Starving yourself is not the way to deal with bad news.' He took her arm. 'Come.'

The brush of his fingers scorched her to the bone. She shook him off. 'Don't touch me.'

He stepped back, his mouth tightening. 'As you wish, Maddalena. But my mother and the food are waiting. You will obey me in this at least.'

She preceded him into the house where Domenica waited to conduct them into the cool dimness of a formal *sala da pranzo*. Long crimson drapes had been half-drawn to exclude the sunlight and, in the centre of the room, a large ceiling fan turned with silent efficiency.

The circular table in some dark wood was set with silver, crystal and exquisite lace mats, and the long sideboard which matched it was almost groaning under the weight of several ornate silver candelabra, a heavily chased antique coffee service, and a range of elegant silver-topped decanters.

It made the huge dining hall at Casa Lupo seem almost rustically simple, thought Maddie as she took the indicated high-backed chair.

After the *antipasti*—a delicious selection of spiced meats, sausages and tiny platters of seafood—came *linguine* served simply with *pesto,* which, as Maddie had learned at Casa Lupo, had been invented in Genoa.

The main course was fish, baked in a sizzling cheese and herb sauce, and this was followed by peaches in red wine.

Domenica was waiting at table, and Maddie fully expected to find one of the courses being served straight into her lap, but the worst that came her way was the usual surly glance.

She managed to eat some of everything put in

front of her, although her usual appetite had deserted her.

Conversation, unsurprisingly, was also fairly stilted. Andrea said little, lost in his thoughts, so it was left to the Contessa to ask civil questions about Maddie's work at Athene and receive equally polite replies.

'I hope your experiences here will not give you a distaste for Italian opera,' the Contessa remarked at last as coffee was served. 'I noticed that you seemed to enjoy "Rigoletto".'

Maddie stared at her, remembering the curtained box. 'You—were there too?'

'*Certamente.* I was as curious to see you, *signorina*, as you were to see me, although for very different reasons. As for the performance, I thought Ernesto Brazzoni lacked that spark of the devil that makes the Duke so interesting—and so attractive to all those unfortunate women.'

Maddie drank some of the rich fragrant brew in front of her. She said coolly, 'Not a trait that holds any appeal for me, I'm afraid. I think a member of the aristocracy should show more discrimination.'

Andrea roused himself from his introspection. He said softly, 'But if he did, Maddalena, there would be no story.'

She lifted her chin. 'And the girl who truly loved

him would be saved from misery and a wretched ending.'

'Ah,' he said, his mouth curling cynically. 'True love. I bow to your greater experience in such a matter.'

The breath caught in her throat. And you, she thought. How much would you have taught me about heartbreak if I'd given myself to you, body and soul? How long has that girl in Viareggio spent lately, wondering where you are? Waiting for you to call?

At which point, Domenica came back into the room. She went straight to Andrea, speaking to him quietly, but Maddie caught the word '*telefonata*' and realised her stomach was churning suddenly in mingled excitement and dread.

Calm down, she told herself. It could be any-thing—some business matter—a problem at the house.

Then watched him get to his feet and pause briefly to place a hand on his mother's shoulder before striding from the room, and knew that it was not just—anything.

The Contessa sat rigidly, staring in front of her, the tension in the room almost tangible as the min-utes ticked endlessly by.

Maddie looked down at her hands, clenched so tightly in her lap that her knuckles were white.

This is the moment you've been waiting for, longing for, said a small stony voice in her head. You should be thinking of your reunion with Jeremy and smiling, bubbling with joy inside at the thought of seeing him again. Of returning to normal. Resuming the preparations for your wedding.

But today has changed all that. Now you no longer know what to expect—except there's bound to be confrontation—fallout. Because you've learned things you'd rather not have known. Stuff you have to try and live with.

And felt herself shiver.

Andrea came back into the room, closing the door behind him.

His voice was quiet, almost flat, without a hint of triumph. 'A visitor has arrived from England and is waiting at the house. It appears he has brought with him the letter we have been waiting for.' A muscle moved in his throat. 'It is over at last.'

There was a silence, then the Contessa's icy control snapped and she burst into tears. Andrea's arms went round her, drawing against his shoulder as he whispered to her in his own language.

Maddie rose silently, went to the door and let

herself out. As she paused in the hall, Domenica reappeared.

'Why are you here?' she demanded aggressively. 'Did Her Excellency invite you to look round her house? I think no.'

'I wish to find a bathroom,' Maddie returned. 'I suppose that is permitted.'

Domenica muttered something under her breath, and led the way upstairs to a spacious room tiled in pale blue and silver.

'I wait here,' she announced, stepping back into the passage.

In case I try to make off with the towels, thought Maddie, trying to derive some humour from the situation, and failing utterly.

She had a strong desire to emulate the Contessa and find release for her confused and troubling emotions in a flood of weeping.

Her legs were trembling so much she had to lean against the marble washbasin, while she splashed cold water over her face and wrists. Her reflection in the mirror above the basin was no comfort either. She looked as white as a ghost, her eyes hunted—haunted.

It was shock, she told herself. Shock mingled with relief that her ordeal was coming to an end at last. That was all.

And when she got to Casa Lupo and found Jeremy waiting for her, she would be fine again, and they'd face the inevitable problems together.

So why was it suddenly so difficult to form an image of him—let alone to remember the sound of his voice, or the feel of his arms around her?

A brief tap on the door made her snap out of her reverie. Domenica was clearly becoming impatient.

'*Uno momento,*' she called back, combing her hair back from her face with shaking fingers and struggling to re-fasten the clip.

'Do you want to search me?' she began as she opened the door, then stopped, her face warming with embarrassment as she saw it was not Domenica but the Contessa waiting outside. 'Oh—I—I'm sorry.'

'There is no need.' The Contessa's eyes were red, but she was back in control. 'My son has asked me to say that he wishes to leave as soon as possible.'

'Yes,' Maddie said, swallowing. 'Yes, of course.'

'And I sent my maid away so that I could speak privately to you,' the older woman added. 'I have an apology to make to you, *signorina.* I thought you must know the true nature of your future father-in-law, but were prepared to overlook this because of his wealth and position. Therefore, in my eyes, you were one of them.'

She paused. 'Having met you, I no longer believe this, and accept that you had a right to know the reason for your involvement, and that you should hear it from me.'

'My relationship with Mr Sylvester has never been easy,' Maddie admitted. 'And now it's going to be more difficult than ever. I—I accept that too.

'But, on the other hand, I've always told myself that I was marrying Jeremy, not his father, and I know my fiancé is just another innocent party in all this.' She gave a determinedly bright smile. 'We can work things out. I'm sure of it.'

There was a brief silence, then: 'Your loyalty is commendable,' said the Contessa, adding wryly, 'and so is Domenica's in a different way. She has always been ferociously devoted to me.'

'I only saw the ferocious bit.' Maddie hesitated. 'Is she like that with all outsiders, or just me?'

'Her grandmother was said to have the sight—the ability to see into the future,' said Floria Valieri. 'It seems she predicted that a fair-haired woman from across the sea would bring about the end of the House of the Wolf. Domenica was convinced from the first that it was you.'

Maddie shook her head. 'She's quite wrong. I'm

sure I won't be the last blonde foreigner to cross Andrea's path.'

She forced another smile. 'I know I made a lot of threats at the start and meant them, but that's all over now.' She took a breath. 'And I promise that I shan't make trouble for him when I get back to London. So you mustn't worry about that.'

'I am grateful for the reassurance.' The Contessa gave her a meditative look. '*Tuttavia, signorina,* I fear it may be too late and the damage may already be done.'

She gave a brief, harsh sigh. 'So be it. And now we must not keep Andrea waiting any longer.'

CHAPTER THIRTEEN

HE WAS IN the hall, pacing restlessly, his face strained and brooding. He came across to his mother, took her hands and kissed them, and then her cheek.

'And now I deal with what remains to be done, Mammina.' He looked down at her searchingly. 'I proceed as we agreed? You have not changed your mind?'

'Justice will be done,' said the Contessa. 'That is what matters. And our decision is made.'

He bent his head in affirmation, and Maddie felt a faint shiver pass through her.

He is Crime. I am Punishment.

She'd thought Andrea didn't know what he'd taken on with Nigel Sylvester. She now saw that the boot was on the other foot.

As they left the villa to walk back to the car, Maddie glanced back and saw a familiar face peering at her from a front window, her clenched fist extended.

'What does this mean?' She demonstrated.

Andrea frowned. 'It is the *mano cornuto*,' he said brusquely. 'Protection against the evil eye. I suppose it is Domenica?'

'Yes, but I think she's being a little over-cautious.' She tried to speak lightly. 'After all, she's never going to see me again.'

'I am sorry she ever saw you at all,' was the harsh return. 'I put her in charge of you because my mother taught her to speak English, and I thought it would make matters easier. I see now that it was a mistake.'

'Your mother's English is wonderful,' she ventured.

'She learned languages as part of her training. She is also fluent in French, and can speak some German.'

She was silent for a moment, then said with constraint, 'If the letter does what you want, do you think she will sing again?'

He shrugged. '*Non lo so.* Who can tell?'

Which closed another conversational avenue, thought Maddie, her throat tightening. But why should that matter when Jeremy was only a relatively short drive away from her and they would be going home together? As soon as I see him, she told herself restlessly, as soon as he takes me in his arms, everything will be all right again. Besides, I can stand up to his father now, which will make our future together so much easier.

I know it.

And she kept whispering these three words under her breath like a mantra as they drove swiftly and silently back to Casa Lupo.

At the house, a strange car was waiting at one side of the drive, its driver leaning against the bonnet and smoking a cigarette.

Eustacio was standing on the steps, his expression frankly anxious, as he watched his employer's car come to a halt. As Andrea left the vehicle, he was greeted by a flood of Italian, and he paused for a clearly soothing word before allowing Maddie to precede him into the house.

In the hall, she paused, staring at the wall of panelling, the final barrier, and heard Andrea just behind her say very quietly, 'Maddalena.'

She had a crazy, terrifying impulse to turn and fling herself into his arms, to beg him to hold her and keep her safe forever, and found herself fighting it with every atom of resolve she possessed.

'My name is Maddie,' she said. 'Maddie Lang. And I'd like to see my fiancé, please.'

Watching him open the door into the *salone,*

Maddie's heart was thudding painfully and she was conscious of a slight feeling of nausea.

She thought, Jeremy's waiting for me but I don't want to go in there. I don't want to face him, yet I must. I must...

Then adjured herself sharply for being a fool, because this was the moment she'd been waiting for over all these long days and nights. This and nothing else...

It had to be.

Head high, she marched past Andrea into the room and stopped dead, her hand flying to her mouth, because the man rising from a chair beside the fireplace was not Jeremy at all but a complete stranger, of more than medium height and corpulent with thinning grey hair and a florid face.

He said, 'You'll be Miss Lang. For a supposed kidnap victim you seem to be kept on a pretty loose rein. Do you know how long I've been waiting?'

Andrea said evenly, 'If we had known of your arrival, *signore,* the inconvenience could have been avoided.'

The newcomer looked him up and down. 'I'm here to make a delivery to a Count Valieri, while you, young lady, pack your things. We're catching an evening flight from Genoa.'

Maddie stiffened, but Andrea was intervening courteously. 'I think your name is Simpson, *signore*. May I welcome you to my home?'

'We don't have time for that,' the older man said sharply. 'My instructions are to do the business and leave with the girl.' He turned to Maddie. 'Hurry up, dear. You've caused enough trouble without making us miss that plane.'

She said in a shaking voice, 'How dare you talk to me like that? And where is Jeremy, my fiancé? Why isn't he here?'

He pursed his lips. 'You think my client would allow him to walk into another extortionist trap? Oh, no, sweetheart. Your little escapade has cost quite enough.

'And I've been retained to collect you, safe and unharmed as promised by your kidnapper and return you to London.'

He opened a briefcase beside his chair and extracted an envelope. 'As for the so-called Count, he gets this in exchange for you. And I want a receipt.'

Andrea's smile was icy. 'I hope you will not object if I check the contents of the envelope before I release Signorina Lang into your custody.'

He took the envelope from the other's reluctant grasp and walked to the window at the far end of the room, standing with his back turned as he scanned its contents.

Maddie stared at the fireplace where a small fire was burning, wishing the cheerful flames could melt the block of ice inside her.

She thought, Supposing—supposing it doesn't say what they want? What he's expecting? What will happen then?

And remembered Floria Valieri's words, 'Justice will be done.'

But he came back looking cool and unruffled, the envelope in his hand.

'Your client has kept his word,' he said. 'I shall keep mine. I will arrange for Signorina Lang's clothes and other possessions to be packed and brought down immediately.'

'I think,' Maddie said coldly and quietly, 'that is for me to decide, so please both of you stop talking about me as if I wasn't here.' She turned to the older man. 'I shall not be travelling with you, Mr Simpson, tonight or at any other time. Explain to your client that I arrived alone and I shall go back alone when I choose to do so, using my own return ticket.'

'Those aren't my client's instructions.'

'You're paid to do his bidding,' said Maddie. 'I, however, am not.' She added crisply, 'And if he

wished me to comply, he should have sent a messenger with a different attitude. Tell him that as
well.'

'But he'll be waiting...'

'And I've been waiting too,' Maddie returned.
'For quite a long time, considering I expected to
be out of here in forty-eight hours at most. Maybe
you should also mention that.'

Mr Simpson turned on Andrea. He seemed to
be swelling visibly. 'This breaks the agreement.'

Andrea shrugged. 'How can that be?' he drawled.
'I have released Signorina Lang. She is no longer
under my control—or that of anyone else, it seems.
Nor can I force her to return with you.' He paused
meditatively. 'You could, I suppose, drag her to
your car, but I would not recommend it.'

'Nor would I,' said Maddie.

'I'm beginning to think you're in this with him,'
Mr Simpson said glaring at her. 'Maybe I should
take that envelope back.'

'Then think again, because you will not get it.'
Andrea's tone was ice. 'Let us not stray into the
realms of fantasy, *signore*. The *signorina* and I met
for the first time on the night she was brought here
and she has been held against her will ever since.
Only two days ago, she risked her safety and her

health by trying to escape. She will rejoin her future husband when she chooses to do so.'

'And what guarantee does he have of that?' Mr Simpson demanded.

'My sworn promise,' Andrea said quietly. 'Which once again he will have to trust.' He crossed to the door and opened it. *'Addio, signore.* I cannot pretend it has been a pleasure.'

Mr Simpson hesitated, as if searching for a reply, then contented himself with grabbing his briefcase and storming out. A moment or two later, his car was heard to roar off down the drive.

Maddie said roundly, 'What an obnoxious little toad.'

Andrea closed the door and walked back to where she was standing. 'Even so, that was not wise, Maddalena.'

She stared at him. 'You think I should have gone with him?'

'You have told me many times that you only wished to be free,' he countered harshly. 'To prove it you ran away. Now it is over, and you have the chance to leave and every reason to do so, but instead you stay. Why?'

The enormity of the question and its implications made her reel inwardly, grasping at straws to answer him. Didn't he know? Hadn't he sensed her emotional turmoil? Guessed the reason for her inner confusion?

'I—I suppose I was a bit thrown.' Her voice was uneven. 'I was so sure that it would be Jeremy here today. That he would come for me himself. I—I was counting on it.'

Which was certainly the truth.

He said flatly, 'I am sorry your faith was not rewarded.'

She swallowed. 'But I'll go tomorrow, if Camillo can be spared to drive me to Genoa. I'll find a hotel there, until I can get a plane home.'

Unless you ask me to stay...

'That will not be necessary. I shall make arrangements for you to be on the next convenient flight tomorrow.' He held out the envelope. 'As this is the reason for your recent ordeal, you should read it.'

He added quietly, 'It will confirm everything you learned earlier today. So take it, Maddalena, *per favore.*'

The single sheet was hand-written, the pen in places almost gouging narrow channels in the expensive paper.

Maddie found she was holding it with her fingertips, as if to avoid contamination as she scanned the closely written lines, beginning 'I, Nigel Walton Sylvester...'

He admitted everything, without excuse or apology. The money had been taken from dormant foreign accounts to finance his private share deals. These high-risk investments had been unsuccessful, and he had not been able to conceal what he had done by repaying the money.

He had realised Tommaso Marchetti's investigation into irregularities in the Milan branch would lead to his disgrace and an inevitable jail sentence. Determined to save himself at all costs when the other man refused to help cover up his illegal activities, he had deliberately laid a false trail, implicating his former friend as the real thief.

In court, it would have been a matter of one man's word against another's and he was confident that the evidence he had fabricated would lead to a conviction, when the case came to trial.

In the event, because of the prison stabbing, this belief was never tested.

But he now declared that Tommaso Marchetti was innocent of all the charges brought against him.

This was followed by his signature and the date.

Maddie drew a deep breath as she handed the letter back. 'Your father was his friend,' she said. 'Yet he doesn't say one word of regret or remorse about his death.'

'The letter was written under protest, Maddalena, not out of decency. He wished only to stop me making public the evidence I already possessed.'

'When—when did he learn about that?'

He shrugged. 'Forgive me, but I do not remember.'

'No?' She smiled bitterly. 'I bet it was when you discovered that he wouldn't lift a finger to get me back, and you needed to exert some real pressure.'

'*Non importa.* He has confessed, and my father has been vindicated at last. That is what matters.'

'But it can't end there,' Maddie protested. 'You have his confession. You must intend to use it.'

'We wished for reparation,' Andrea said simply. 'He has made it. Also, he has had to refuse the great honour intended for him. For such a man that is punishment enough, I think. So now, I will take the action agreed with my mother.'

He tore the letter across, walked to the fireplace and dropped the pieces on to the flickering flames.

'Oh God,' Maddie said appalled, and would have made a grab for them if he hadn't restrained her. 'What have you done? Have you gone completely mad? You've destroyed your most valuable piece of evidence.'

'But how will he ever know?' Andrea asked quietly. 'Unless you tell him.'

She said slowly, '"Justice will be done."' She sighed. 'I understand now what your mother meant.' She paused. 'It—it's been quite a day. I think I'll go to my room for a while.'

'As you wish.' He crossed the room and opened the door for her. 'Can you remember your way, or shall I send for Luisa?'

'I can manage.' She glanced at him under her lashes. 'By now I could probably find your hidden doors, if I was pushed.'

'Or those you have seen, at least.' His smile was swift and polite.

Treating her, she thought, as if she was a guest—nothing more. And a guest who had outstayed her welcome. But then what else had she really expected...?

He added, 'Until later, then.'

And Maddie nodded, smiling back, and left him, her hands clenched by her sides to conceal the fact that they were trembling.

When she reached the suite, she went into her room and threw herself face downwards across the bed, pressing herself into the mattress as if it might open up and hide her.

She thought, 'What am I going to do? Oh God, what am I going to do?'

Somehow she had to get through the rest of the

day—and the night—without revealing the seething turmoil within her. To deal with the stranger that Andrea had suddenly become.

It was almost better when he'd been her enemy, she thought. Then, at least, he had looked at her as if she was human.

No, she amended quickly and guiltily. He'd looked at her as if she was a woman. She'd sensed it from the beginning, responded to it, at first against her will, then quite deliberately in an attempt to ameliorate a dangerous situation.

But only to be caught in her own trap, finding herself drawn to him and wholly unable to resist his attraction. This urgent, aching need he'd somehow awoken in her. And which he'd seemed to share.

Yet now...

She buried her involuntary moan in the pillow.

I never meant it to happen, she whispered silently, as if placating some unseen malevolent force. And I should have believed him when he said it was over. Should have made myself leave with the hateful Simpson.

Because she knew now that nothing—*nothing*—could be worse than inhabiting this—limbo she'd been consigned to.

At last she got up wearily, loosened her hair, removed her skirt and top and, after a brief trip to the bathroom to wash her face and hands in cool water, slid under the coverlet and tried to sleep.

It was not easy. Image after image chased through her mind, and all of them Andrea—devouring her with his eyes as she descended the stairs towards him, kneeling to attend to her blistered feet, and, above all, pleasuring her with such potent lingering sweetness that she ached at its memory.

Memories that were all she would have to take with her when she left.

Eventually, the pictures in her head began to blur and slip away and with them, if only for a little while, went the tension, the hurt and the unspoken yearning as she slept.

There were shadows in the room when she opened her eyes, but as she sat up she realised there was light coming from the bathroom together with the sound of the bath filling, and the next moment Luisa appeared in the doorway.

She checked. '*Scusi, signorina.*' She indicated her watch. '*E l'ora di cena.*'

She went to the closet and extracted the black dress, but Maddie shook her head.

'No, *grazie*. I will choose—*decidere.*'

Luisa's expression as she hung the dress back in the closet plainly asked 'What choice?' But she ducked her head in assent and left Maddie to her own devices.

Her sleep had done her good, she thought, as she went into the bathroom. She had woken, seeing things much more clearly, knowing herself far better than she'd done an hour or so ago.

And, as a result, she'd reached a decision. One last throw of the dice, she told herself. Make—or break.

She sniffed at each of the array of bath essences and picked one with the scent of clove carnations, adding a generous capful to the steaming water.

After she'd bathed and dried herself, she used the matching body lotion rubbing it lightly and sensuously into her skin. She gave a slight grimace as the mirrored reflection of her nakedness showed that she was still bruised from her recent adventure, although the grazes were healing well.

But there was no time for the marks to fade, she thought, as she returned to the bedroom. She had to act now. Tonight.

Besides he already knew what she looked like without her clothes, bruises and all, she reminded herself, her skin warming at the recollection.

She opened the adjoining closet and took the black nightgown and robe from the rail. As she slipped the gown over her head, the delicate fabric, so sheer it was like a dark mist, touched her like a caress.

It hid almost nothing, of course. But wasn't that exactly why he'd chosen it? And if she'd worn it the first time to throw his challenge back in his face, this time she intended it to be total enticement, she thought with satisfaction as she slid her arms into the sleeves of the robe, and fastened its buttons.

She brushed her hair into its usual smooth fall, before darkening her lashes and emphasising the curve of her mouth with her favourite soft coral lustre.

This time, she made her own way downstairs, underlining her new status as guest rather than prisoner. She walked to the panelling, found the hidden catch and silently opened the door into the *salone*.

Andrea was standing by the fireplace, staring down at the small heap of glowing logs.

Maddie took a deep breath. 'You see?' she announced. 'I actually managed the door.'

He turned abruptly, glass in hand, standing as if transfixed as Maddie walked towards him, a faint smile playing about her lips.

'My compliments.' He did not return the smile. 'You will be pleased to hear that your flight to

London tomorrow has been booked, and that Camillo will drive you to Genoa. Perhaps you can be ready by noon.'

She was not deceived by the implied dismissal or the formal tone in which it was uttered. She had seen the swift flare in his eyes, and the involuntary movement of a muscle in his throat and knew that the significance of her attire—or lack of it—had not been lost on him.

She said with equal civility, 'That's very kind of you.'

'*Al contrario.* We shall both be relieved when our lives return to normal, and I was anxious that no more time should be wasted.' He paused. 'May I get you a drink?'

'Some white wine, please,' she said, slightly unnerved by what he had said. This, she thought, was not going to plan.

She took the glass he brought her and raised it in a toast. 'To the future—whatever it may bring.'

'For you there seems little doubt.' He raised his own glass. Drank. 'You will marry the man you love. Your faith in him has not wavered.'

'Apart from today,' she said in a low voice. 'When he didn't come to fetch me.'

'A small misunderstanding, soon forgiven I am sure.'

She stared at him. 'But you said in his place, you'd storm the place to get me back.'

'I said a good many things, none of which now matter.' He briskly finished his whisky and set down the empty glass on the dining table, at which, Maddie noticed with sudden disquiet, only one place had been set.

He added, 'And now you must excuse me, Maddalena. I am dining elsewhere tonight. I may not return before you go tomorrow, so please accept my best wishes for a safe journey and a happy arrival. What is it your Shakespeare says—that journeys end in lovers' meetings? I hope it will be true for you.'

He took her nerveless hand and bowed over it. *'Addio, mia bella.* Your *fidanzato* is a fortunate man.'

Stunned, she watched him walk to the door. She said in a voice she didn't recognise, 'I don't understand. You're leaving me to spend this evening— our last time together—alone?'

His voice seemed to reach her across a million light years of space. 'There is no "together", Maddalena. How could there be? And we can part without regret. One day you will thank me for that, believe me.'

'Will you at least tell me where are you going?'

He paused. Shrugged. 'To Viareggio, *carissima,* as I often do.' He added softly, 'But I think you already know that.'

And went.

CHAPTER FOURTEEN

'MY GOD, DARLING,' Jeremy said huskily. 'It's been absolute hell on bloody earth. I felt I was living through a nightmare.'

Maddie looked down at the glitter of the diamonds, now restored to her left hand. She said quietly, 'It wasn't exactly a walk in the park for me, either.'

But her nightmare, she thought, had begun forty-eight hours ago and was still continuing.

Jeremy shuddered. 'You must have been terrified.'

'At first,' she said. 'Then I got angry.'

'Although, as my father said, you were never in any real danger. It wasn't as if you'd been grabbed by the Mafia.' He lowered his voice confidentially. 'In fact, I gather it was all rather a storm in a teacup.'

'Really?' She kept her voice even. 'I didn't see it like that.'

'Perhaps not,' he said. 'Yet here you are, home, safe, and all in one piece.'

In one piece, Maddie echoed in silent incredulity. Are you blind? Can't you see that I've fallen apart? That I'm in bits?

Jeremy was speaking again, 'I suppose you've told your family—your boss—everyone—what happened to you.'

'No,' she said. 'My aunt and uncle, the girls, Todd—they all think I've been running round Northern Italy trying to track my lost soprano, and have now admitted defeat.' She gave him a steady look. 'I thought that was best.'

'Absolutely. It solves a lot of problems—awkward questions and stuff.' He shook his head. 'After all, the whole thing was utterly ludicrous. Completely OTT. All this panic and uproar just to get Dad to exonerate some long-dead former employee from a richly deserved charge of fraud. Well, who could believe that?'

'Who indeed?' Maddie agreed ironically. 'But if it was such a trivial matter, why did it take so long to fix it?'

He looked uncomfortable. 'Well, darling, it's the kind of situation that could easily be misconstrued. Dad had the bank's reputation to consider.'

'Yes, of course,' she said. 'Silly me.'

'And what's it to do with this Valieri guy anyway? He must be totally barking.'

'No.' Maddie considered for a moment. 'Just— single-minded and very determined.'

'Well, Trevor Simpson didn't see him like that. His report was very different.'

'I can imagine.'

He hesitated. 'For one thing, it mentions that when he arrived, you were out driving round the countryside in Valieri's company.'

Maddie turned her instinctive flinch into a shrug. 'What of it?'

'And then you refused to let Simpson bring you back.' He paused. 'You must see that it looks— odd.'

'Actually, I don't. I was offered a "get out of jail free" card for a few hours.' *Or free apart from the bitter cost in heartache, shame and regret.*

'I was going stir-crazy,' she went on. 'So I accepted.'

She added crisply, 'And I found your Mr Simpson quite loathsome. Is that sufficient explanation?'

'A bit of a rough diamond, perhaps,' Jeremy said stiffly. 'But Dad finds him useful and efficient.' He took her hand. 'I'm not trying to upset you, truly, but this is a difficult situation for me—and clearly I'm not handling it very well.

'But I have to say that meeting in a wine bar after work isn't the sort of romantic reunion I'd hoped for.' He put his lips close to her ear. 'Let's get out of here and go to the flat. Dad's promised we'll have it to ourselves.'

Maddie controlled a sudden shiver. She said, 'Jeremy, I can't. Not yet. I've been through an ordeal. I—I need time.'

He sat back, his mouth tightening in obvious disappointment. 'Which is something else we need to talk about. My father suggests that our wedding should be brought forward. That we have a quiet ceremony quite soon, and a big celebratory party as planned on the original date.'

'Bring the wedding forward?' she said slowly. 'But why?'

Jeremy looked uncomfortable again. 'He hopes it will make you feel more—settled. Besides, it's only what you once claimed you wanted,' he added defensively. 'Let's elope, you said. Special licence and a couple of witnesses.'

'Which you refused.'

'Surely I'm allowed to change my mind.'

'Yes,' Maddie said. 'But so am I. And I think the previous arrangements should stand.' She paused. 'Needing some recovery time doesn't make me a basket case.'

He took her hand again. 'Sweetheart, can't you understand that, after what happened, I don't want to wait any longer?'

She bit her lip. 'I think I've been subjected to enough pressure just recently. This is a major decision, Jeremy, and I won't be rushed.'

'Rushed?' he repeated as if the word was new to him. 'God, Maddie, we're engaged to be married. You've promised to be my wife. Does it really matter if it happens sooner rather than later?'

Logic suggested that it didn't. Gut instinct advised her to stick to her guns.

She said, 'Tell me something. Why didn't you bring that letter to Italy yourself?'

'I wanted to, darling, believe me. But it was—tricky. You must see that.'

'Tricky?' she repeated. 'What's tricky about a storm in a teacup? Be honest, Jeremy. Your father said no, and you wouldn't go against him. Not even if it meant being reunited with me a few days sooner.'

'It was natural for him to be concerned.'

'I wish he'd been equally concerned for me. I could have been free so much earlier.' She paused. 'Is that why he didn't want me to go to Italy—because he was afraid the past might come back to haunt him?'

'Of course not,' he said quickly. 'It was just some long-forgotten petty crime. He simply didn't wish to be forced into a number of untruthful and potentially damaging admissions about it.

'But, of course, your safety and well-being were paramount, so, in the end, he put his name to that tissue of lies. And that wasn't all either. He had to ask not to be put forward for a life peerage. This hit him hard, but he said no sacrifice was too great.'

Maddie thought of the Contessa collapsing into a flood of tears because the honour of the man she loved had been vindicated at last. Of Andrea dropping the letter into the flames as if it was coated in slime.

But she supposed Jeremy, the devoted only son, could hardly be blamed for believing anything his father told him.

Jeremy's voice became quiet, almost casual. 'Tell me, my sweet, did the Valieri man ever say what he planned to do with it? Dad's letter, I mean? He went to enough trouble to get hold of it, so he must have something in mind.'

He burnt it...

She almost spoke the words, but at the last moment something stopped her.

She said, 'He was hardly likely to confide in me.' And paused. 'Why do you ask?'

'For God's sake, darling, isn't it obvious? The bloody thing's out there like a time bomb waiting to go off.'

Maddie said carefully, 'Perhaps just having it is enough and he doesn't mean to use it.'

Jeremy's mouth hardened into an unpleasant line. 'Sure—and watch out for flying pigs. Do you really think a bastard like that can be trusted?'

'My experience of bastards,' Maddie said, 'is rather limited.'

He sighed. 'Darling, this is why I want us to get married as quickly as possible. Maybe the notion of a man wanting to cherish and protect his wife is an old-fashioned one. If so, I'm an old-fashioned man and proud of it. So why make me wait?'

Maddie took a deep breath. 'Maybe because of an inbuilt conviction that marriage is an equal partnership and that I'm quite able to take care of myself,' she retorted.

'Not,' Jeremy said, 'according to the evidence of the past few weeks.'

'But I wasn't the real target,' Maddie pointed out quietly. 'It was my association with your family that really exposed me to risk.'

'And is this why you're refusing to marry me?'

'I haven't refused,' she said. 'I just haven't made up my mind.'

'Well, we can discuss it at the weekend,' said Jeremy. 'Dad suggested we should go somewhere quiet and secluded together.'

Maddie wondered dispassionately how many times Nigel Sylvester had been mentioned since they'd first brought their drinks to this corner table.

She said quietly, 'I'm afraid that isn't possible. I've already arranged to stay with my aunt and uncle.'

He looked dismayed. 'Can't you see them another time? Surely if you explained we need time together they'd understand.'

'Perhaps, but I owed them a visit before I went away,' Maddie returned. 'And anyway a few days at home will give me time to think. Then I promise you'll have your answer.'

She also refused more wine and dinner at her favourite restaurant. 'Can I take a rain check?' Sensing his annoyance, she gave him a placatory smile. 'I haven't been sleeping too well since I got back, and I need an early night.' *Alone...*

Outside the bar, Jeremy signalled to a taxi. As it drew up to the kerb, he took Maddie's face in his hands and looked into her eyes.

He said in a low voice, 'I hate myself for asking this, but I must. This Valieri—I need to know what happened while you were together. Oh God, Maddie did he use you—force himself on you?'

She met his gaze, telling herself she should be thankful that she could. Glad that she could be truthful about this at least.

'No,' she said quietly. 'He never did. On the contrary.' She swallowed. 'I was simply part of a business transaction. Does that reassure you?'

'I suppose it has to.' He bent his head and kissed her, and Maddie made herself respond to the pressure of his lips.

'We're together again,' he whispered, as he put her into the cab. 'Back where we belong. I know everything's going to be all right, and I'll be waiting for your answer.'

As the taxi drove off, Maddie glanced back and saw him still standing on the edge of the kerb, eyes narrowed, face frowning as he watched her go, and had the strangest impression she was looking at a stranger.

But then nothing in the past two days had seemed quite real.

Not from the moment she'd fled from the *salone* back to her room, ripping off the robe and nightgown and leaving them in a crumpled heap on the floor. Crawling into the bed like a small animal seeking its lair.

But not to sleep. Instead she'd lain, staring into the darkness, counting the hours. Twice she'd got up, stumbling over to the door to his room and standing there, her fingers clasping the handle but afraid to turn it.

Wondering which would be worse—to find the bed unoccupied or risk another rejection.

When he'd said it was over, she hadn't realised he also meant she had served her purpose. That at best she had been a challenge but now she had become an inconvenience to be dispensed with as soon as possible. A line had been drawn and her pathetic ill-judged attempt to cross it had simply ended in her own humiliation.

In the morning, all the other possessions she'd brought to Italy were waiting in the hall, as she came downstairs with her travel bag. Nothing had been overlooked.

Removing all trace of me, she thought, and the hurt of that was not assuaged by discovering at the airport that she'd been upgraded to first class.

Waiting for the flight to be called, she'd rung Aunt Fee, Todd and her flatmates warning them of her imminent return.

But not Jeremy. She wasn't ready to face him. Not immediately.

I've too much to hide, she'd told herself, and I need some leeway.

Because she was too muddled, too emotionally bruised to be making major decisions about her future. Her days at the House of the Wolf had thrown her entire life into chaos and somehow she needed to pick up the threads of her existence and weave them back into a pattern that made sense.

Because, with the only certainty in her reeling world, she knew that if Andrea Valieri had taken her when she offered herself, she would not have left.

That she would have given herself, body and soul, for good or ill, and for as long as he wanted.

And the knowledge terrified her.

But now she had a whole weekend of peace and quiet in which to pull herself together, close the door on the past, and rebuild her future. The real future she had so nearly betrayed.

'Back where we belong,' Jeremy had said, and he was right. Because that was surely what she had to aim for. To remember, to the exclusion of all else, why she'd fallen in love with him, and agreed to be his wife. Because nothing else mattered.

After all, it would be wrong to assign any real blame in the Marchetti affair to him. He wasn't responsible for something his father had done before he was born and lied about ever since.

Essentially, she needed to create a strong marriage which would act as a counterweight to Nigel Sylvester's influence. It wouldn't be easy, because she couldn't destroy Jeremy's illusions about his father, but it must happen if they were to have any chance of happiness.

And I'll make it happen, she vowed silently.

Sally and Trisha had gone to the cinema, so she had the flat to herself when she got back. There was quiche and salad waiting in the fridge, so she ate a quick supper and decided to look through some of the emails that had accumulated on her personal laptop while she'd been absent.

As she scrolled down, the name 'Janet Gladstone' leapt out at her. My wedding dress, she thought, faintly puzzled. I wasn't expecting to hear from her.

She clicked on the message, and sat, staring in disbelief. 'It was a rush,' it read. 'But I've managed to get it finished. Please let me know when you can come for a final fitting.'

For a moment, Maddie felt as if a cold hand had touched her skin. Did Mrs Gladstone practise clairvoyance in her spare time? she wondered. Because this was more than odd. In fact, it was seriously weird, and distinctly premature.

'What a surprise,' she wrote back, after some thought. 'I'll see you at the weekend.'

And I'll be asking some questions at the same time, she thought as she pressed Send.

'It's perfect,' Maddie said almost reverently, letting the wild silk shimmer round her as she turned slowly in front of the full-length mirror. 'Beautiful. And it needs no alterations at all.' She shook her head. 'Amazing. Thank you so much.'

Janet Gladstone beamed with satisfaction. 'Not completely finished. Just one last stitch needed in the hem before you leave for the church. I like the old superstitions.'

Before I leave for the church, thought Maddie, trying to imagine it. To see herself walking up the aisle on Uncle Patrick's arm to where Jeremy waited. To feel her heart lift as he turned to smile at her.

But this inner picture was strangely blurred, and, as she tried to focus, it wavered and vanished.

As the dress was wrapped in sheets of tissue then carefully encased in its plastic carrier, Maddie asked her question.

'Mrs Gladstone, why did you think this was a rush job? The date I gave you is still weeks away.'

'But Mrs Sylvester told me that date no longer applied. She said that she was calling on your behalf to warn me that the wedding would now be much earlier, and that the order would be cancelled if I couldn't finish the dress in the time available.'

She added, looking anxious, 'I hope I haven't got it wrong, but she seemed so definite.'

'Well, the mistake isn't yours,' Maddie said lightly. 'And what really matters is that I have a wonderful dress.'

She paid the bill and took the dress carrier back to the parking area, placing it carefully across the rear seat of Aunt Fee's car.

She'd intended to go straight home, but when she reached the crossroads, she turned left, heading for Fallowdene.

The housekeeper who answered the door agreed that Mrs Sylvester was at home, and conducted her to the drawing room where Esme was lounging on a sofa reading 'Vogue', a tray of coffee on the table in front of her.

'Madeleine,' she said. 'To what do I owe this unexpected pleasure?' She put down her magazine and waved her to the opposite sofa. 'Mrs Ferguson, please bring another cup.'

'Thank you, but I don't want any coffee.' Maddie paused. 'I've just collected my wedding dress, and I'd like to know why you wanted it finished in such a tearing hurry—and in my absence.'

Esme Sylvester's elegant brows rose. 'The Gladstone woman's actually managed it? How unexpectedly efficient. But I was just the messenger. And a very surprised one, let me tell you.'

'What do you mean?'

She shrugged. 'I didn't think there was going to be a wedding. Neither my husband nor my stepson like having their express wishes ignored, and Jeremy wants a wife who'll do as she's told and fall into line when required. Your Italian trip was quite the last straw.

'But then you were kidnapped, and they had to think again.'

She paused. 'If it had been only about money, they'd never have paid, of course, whatever the kidnappers had threatened. Some statement would have been issued about it being morally reprehensible to yield to blackmail.

'But this, of course, was far worse. This was loss of face. Potential ruin.

'Which is why they had to get you home, and why Jeremy has to sweep you off your feet and into instant matrimony. Because, my dear Madeleine, you now know far too much about the Tommaso Marchetti unpleasantness, and they need those particular facts kept safely in the family.'

Maddie's lips felt stiff. 'You—and Jeremy both know the truth?'

'Naturally.' Esme sounded almost bored. 'Jeremy and his father have no secrets from each other. And, unlike you, I never had any illusions about the man I was going to marry. But the rewards have more than compensated for any passing moral qualms. Will you be able to say the same?'

'I don't believe any of this,' Maddie said desperately. 'You're simply saying these things to make trouble, because you've never liked me.'

Esme smiled cynically. 'You mean Jeremy hasn't already questioned you about what the Valieri man intends to do with his information? Whether he can be trusted to keep his word about Nigel's confession?'

'How—how did you know that?'

'Because, my naïve child, I know the Sylvesters and you don't—or not yet, anyway. And until they get an answer, they won't stop asking.'

She paused. 'And I'm trying to do you a favour here, because you've no idea what you're getting into.'

She gave a short laugh. 'You always made it so

transparently clear you were planning to prise Jeremy lovingly from his father's grasp. But that will never happen, because, whatever you may choose to believe, Jeremy is no longer the boy you fell in love with years ago, but his father's own son.'

She lowered her voice confidentially. 'In fact, I can see a time when Nigel will learn from him. And I'm not at all sure you'll be able to cope with that, however rich you become. You see, we're so very different, you and I.'

'Yes,' Maddie said quietly. 'Yes, we are.' She eased the diamond ring from her left hand and put it on the table. 'Thank you. It's been—illuminating. You see I'd almost convinced myself that Jeremy needed me.'

'Oh, no,' Esme said softly. 'Those two only need each other.'

Maddie was never sure how she got out of the house and back into the car. And of the journey home, she could only remember pulling over on to a verge somewhere and kneeling on the grass being violently sick.

And when the paroxysms were over, she sat up, knowing she was absolved from guilt and heart searching, and half-laughing, half-crying with the relief of it. Knowing too that being completely and utterly alone was so much better than settling for less than second best.

And that, somehow, she could learn to live with that.

CHAPTER FIFTEEN

WHAT TOOK MADDIE slightly aback was the general lack of surprise over the news of her broken engagement. Uncle Patrick murmured that they'd 'often wondered', while Aunt Fee merely whisked away the wedding dress, and produced one of her sumptuous roast duck dinners.

Trisha and Sally took her clubbing, and Todd, with his usual single-mindedness, said he welcomed the news if it meant she would not be leaving any time soon.

And no-one asked her if she was sure she was doing the right thing.

What did they see that I didn't? Maddie wondered, but decided not to enquire.

All the opposition came from Jeremy, who laid siege to her, with texts, emails, armfuls of flowers and visits to the office and the flat, with pleas to 'talk things over, my darling, before it's too late'.

To all of which, she replied quietly and firmly that there was nothing to discuss. Her decision had been made once and for all, and she intended to treat the past as a closed book.

The flowers she took to a local hospice. Her conversation with Esme she kept strictly to herself.

And if she seemed quiet, with a propensity for staring into space, lost in thoughts that were clearly not happy—well, that was surely natural after a broken engagement. So people drew the obvious conclusions, and tactfully forbore to ask questions that she would have found impossible to answer with any degree of truth, if at all.

Time passed slowly, turned into one week, then two, and if her days were easier than her nights, then that was something she admitted only to herself.

Work continued to be her salvation. She and a colleague were researching material for a programme on people whose newly discovered talents had changed their lives. They'd already talked to a roofing engineer who'd learned to play the clarinet and was now performing regularly with a jazz band, a security guard whose watercolours had found a market in a London gallery, while Maddie had just arranged to go to Oxford to interview a retired female academic who'd written an explosively bloodthirsty thriller, when Todd emerged from his office, his eyes popping with excitement.

He said, 'Remember your wild goose chase to Italy? Well, the goose has been found. Floria Bartrando has made contact, would you believe, and she's willing to talk to us.'

For a moment, Maddie felt as if she'd been turned to stone. When she could speak, she said, 'Well good luck to whoever does it.'

Todd stared at her. 'For heaven's sake, Maddie, it's you. She's asked for you by name.'

Maddie shook her head. 'I can't do it, Todd. I—I can't possibly go back to Italy. Please don't ask me to explain.'

'But she's not in Italy.' He slapped a triumphant hand on Maddie's desk. 'She's here in London, staying at the Mayfair Royal hotel, Suite Fourteen, and she'll see you this evening at half seven. How about that?'

She took a breath. 'I suggest you send Holly. I have plans for tonight.'

Todd gave her a level look. 'Then change them. I've told you—it's you she wants to see, and no-one else.' He looked at her pale mutinous face and sighed. 'God, I'll never understand women. You're gone for days on end looking for her, and now she's turned up you don't want to know. I thought you'd be turning cartwheels.

'Well, this is your project, honey, so—whatever

the problem—deal with it.' And he went back into his office and banged the door.

She wanted to go after him—to scream, 'It's not a problem, it's a nightmare.' Except that would involve her in explanations she could not afford to make.

'I'm in the wrong job for secrets,' she muttered under her breath.

She achieved little for the rest of the day, and went home early, pleading a headache. 'Take some ibuprofen,' Todd called after her. 'Make sure you're on top form for seven-thirty.' And his tone made clear it was an order rather than a suggestion.

She dressed down deliberately for the interview—straight grey skirt, plain white blouse, low-heeled black shoes—and pulled her hair back from her face, fastening it severely at the nape of her neck with a black ribbon.

Making it clear to the Contessa that she was no longer the girl her son had brought to Portofino.

The Mayfair Royal was an old-fashioned hotel, with no canned music or loud voices in its hushed and spacious foyer, luxuriously decked out in mahogany and marble.

A polite receptionist confirmed to Maddie that she was expected, and directed her to the lift.

As Maddie emerged on the first floor, a thin grey-haired man was waiting for her.

'Signorina Lang.' He gave her a kind smile. 'My name is Guido Massimo. Will you come with me, please?'

She walked beside him, her feet sinking into the thick carpet, waiting as he produced the key card for Suite Fourteen and opened the door, standing back politely to allow her to precede him.

Maddie stepped into an elegant sitting room, furnished in shades of blue. Glancing round her, she supposed that the double doors to her left and right led to the bedrooms, while ahead of her, a pair of tall windows, giving access to a wrought iron balcony, admitted the fading sunlight of the early June evening.

Behind her, she heard the door close softly, and, turning, realised that Mr Massimo had not accompanied her into the room and that she was alone.

So who will be making the grand entrance? she wondered, mentally bracing herself. Floria Bartrando or the Contessa Valieri?

But when the left hand bedroom door opened, she stood transfixed, her eyes widening endlessly in disbelief as Andrea walked into the room, lean in a sombre dark suit, his shirt open at the throat, his silk tie pulled loose. He paused, hands on hips, tight-lipped, the golden eyes brooding as he looked at her.

He said, 'So you came. I was not sure that you would.'

'I am here,' she said, recovering her breath, 'to talk to your mother. No other reason.' She looked past him, proud of the chill steadiness of her voice. Thankful, too, for her sedate choice of clothing in such marked contrast to the little she'd been wearing at their last confrontation. A memory that made her want to die inside all over again.

'So,' she went on, 'where is she, please?'

'She is visiting friends outside London. She will return tomorrow.'

She swallowed. 'In that case, so shall I.'

'I cannot force you to stay,' he said. His fleeting smile was wry. 'Much as I might wish to do so. But before you go, answer me one question. Is it true that you are no longer engaged to Sylvester's son?'

She flushed. 'That is not your concern.'

'Then let us make it so,' he said. 'I have travelled a long way, Maddalena, to hear your reply.'

'Then you've wasted your time, *signore*.'

'Hope,' he said, 'is never wasted.'

On her way to the door, she turned. 'Hope?' she repeated incredulously. 'What can you possibly be hoping for?'

He said softly, 'Why, for you, *carissima*, if you are no longer promised to the man you left me for.' He took a step towards her. 'You by my side, in my arms, in my bed. Mine completely.'

Her outer tension had not relaxed, but she was trembling inside with shame and anger. And an irrational sense of disappointment.

'How very flattering,' she said savagely. 'So I'll be your girl in London as opposed to the ones in Genoa—Turin—Rome—or any bloody where. No doubt the list is endless. Is that what you're suggesting? Because the answer's no.'

'Do not insult yourself, or me, Maddalena. I do not pretend there have not been women in my life. I am not a eunuch.' His eyes met hers directly, compellingly. 'But, since I met you, no-one. I swear it.' He paused. 'It was—impossible.'

'You're conveniently forgetting your lady friend in Viareggio.' Maddie flung back her head.

He said quietly, 'I visited Giulia once, to say goodbye. She deserved that courtesy.'

'But you went back to her,' she said. 'The night before I left. You told me so.'

'No, *mia cara*. I used that as an excuse. *Infatti*, I drove to Trimontano and stayed alone at the hotel where you had your reservation, in the room where you would have slept.'

276 COUNT VALIERI'S PRISONER

He shook his head. 'I wanted you so badly, my sweet one, that I did not dare spend another night under the same roof with you, or find you still there in the morning.'

'If that's true,' Maddie whispered, 'then why— why did you want to send me away?'

'In order to fulfil my bargain with the Sylvesters.' His voice was suddenly harsh. 'Because I had promised on my honour that I would do so, even though it was like tearing the heart out of my body.

'And I knew if I took you—enjoyed the sweetness you were offering—that I would break my word and never let you go.' He spread his hands almost helplessly. 'And I had no guarantee that you would want to stay, even if we'd become lovers. Persuading you to give yourself for one night is very different to asking you to be with me forever.'

He added more gently, 'And from the beginning, time after time, you told me all you wanted was to return to England and the man you were to marry. So, to have you and then lose you again if you realised that your heart truly belonged with him— that had all the makings of a special kind of hell.

'So I sent you back to him—my enemy that you loved—to find your real happiness—the happiness you believed in—and told myself I must learn to live without you. And that too was hell, especially when I learned you were once again wearing your ring, and preparing for your wedding.'

She said wonderingly, 'How did you know that?'

His mouth twisted ruefully. 'Because in spite of all my brave intentions, I could not release you. Could not say, "This, too, is over."

'You might be separated from me forever, but I still needed to know what you were doing—how you looked—if you were indeed happy. And I still had the means to find out.'

He saw the shock in her face and flung up a hand. 'Ah, *mia cara*, I am not proud of this. But I was desperate—desperate to prove that you, with your courage and your strength, could not commit your life to such a man.

'As before, I devoured every scrap of information that came to me about you, but this time for very different reasons. And I suffered.'

He shook his head, 'Holy Madonna, I did not know such pain existed. That this was what love could do. I realised then that I had been insane to put my given word before what I felt for you, especially when I was dealing with a family themselves without honour,' he added grimly.

'I told myself that instead of sending you back to them, I should have gone on my knees to you and begged you to stay with me for the rest of our lives. To love me and be my wife.'

He paused, and she saw the naked vulnerability in his face. The fear and yearning in his eyes.

He said in a low voice, 'The good God knows I have given you no reason to care for me, Maddalena, but perhaps, if I am patient, you could learn. I ask only for that chance, my sweet one. The chance to hope.'

He took another step. 'Do I have that chance? Say something, even if it is again "no".'

A smile trembled on her lips. 'You haven't given me much opportunity to speak.' She took a deep breath. 'When you left as you did, I—I was devastated. I felt ashamed because I'd made a fool of myself, and guilty because, in doing so, I'd betrayed Jeremy. And I told myself he didn't deserve that because he wasn't responsible for what his father had done, and probably didn't even know about it.

'I wanted to make amends to him, to start over and recapture what we'd once had. But I couldn't. Because I wasn't the same person. But neither was he, and I realised that perhaps I'd never really known him. Just seen what I wanted to see. Believed what I wanted to believe.

'As I did when I first met you.'

'*Carissima*...'

'No,' she said softly. 'Let me finish, my darling. Since I came back, I haven't been living, I've been existing. And I also thought I had nothing to hope for. That all I would ever have was loneliness and regret. But here you are—like a miracle. And it makes no sense, because we hardly know each other, and maybe we'll both need patience, but if you truly want me, I'm yours.'

Andrea repeated, on a shaken laugh, 'If I want you? If…?' He took one long stride and she was wrapped in his arms, his mouth locked to hers in a deep and passionate kiss. She yielded rapturously, pressing closer against his body as if she wished to be absorbed into him, flesh, blood and bone.

He muttered hoarsely, 'So much for patience.' Then lifting her into his arms, he carried her into his bedroom.

She expected to be taken quickly, their mutual hunger swiftly appeased, and would have given herself without reserve to his urgency.

Only she was wrong. Because suddenly it seemed there was all the time in the world for them to savour every delicious, intimate minute. For her to discover that his hands were gentle and unhurried as he dealt with the fastenings of her clothing, smiling his delight into her eyes as he uncovered her completely. Whispering his encouragement as she began, shyly, to undress him in turn.

At last knowing the joy of his naked body against hers as she lay in his arms. The remembered pleasure of his fingers caressing her breasts, his tongue liquid fire as he teased her hardening nipples. The accompaniment of slow, sweet kisses as he stroked her belly and her slackening eager thighs. The flurried excitement of her breathing as his hand slid between her legs, pushing into her heated wetness while one fingertip played with her tiny engorged mound, making her entire body clench with aching desire.

And she was touching him too, running her hands along his shoulders, across his chest, and down over the flat abdomen to clasp the power and strength of his arousal, her fingers moving delicately, provocatively from the base of the rigid staff to its tip, until he groaned his pleasure aloud.

But when Andrea moved over her, lifting her towards him to enter her, she tensed involuntarily and he paused, his eyes searching her face.

'What is wrong? You don't want this?'

'Yes—oh, yes.' She hesitated, then said in a rush, 'But I'm scared.'

'That I'll hurt you?' His surprise was evident. 'I promise I will not.'

'Not that. Scared of disappointing you. Of not giving you what you expect.'

'Ah,' he said softly, his eyes tender. 'And if I tell you that I am also nervous because for the first time I am making love to the girl I love and her happiness means everything to me —what then?'

Her mouth curved into a smile. 'Then maybe I should stop fussing—and be happy.'

'I think so,' he said, and eased his way slowly and gently into her body, filling her. And she took him, deeply and completely, all inhibitions flown, as if all her life she had been waiting for this moment. And for him.

She raised her legs, locking them round him, responding to every potent, fluid thrust, feeling with astonishment the sharp irresistible build of sensation from the innermost depths of her womanhood. Until all control slipped away, leaving her lost—consumed in a spiral of mindless agonising rapture.

Heard Andrea call out to her, his voice hoarse and almost desperate, as he shuddered into his own scalding release.

Afterwards, when the world had stopped reeling, they lay quietly together, their sweat-dampened bodies still joined, Andrea's head pillowed on her breasts.

And heard him whisper, 'You are mine and I am yours' against her skin.

Later, between slow, sweet kisses, they talked.

So,' he said. 'We get married at once. As soon as arrangements can be made.'

Maddie put her lips to the pulse in his throat. 'Are you sweeping me off my feet, *signore*?'

'I think I must, *signorina*.' There was faint rue-fulness in his tone. 'I did not use protection when we loved, as I should have done.'

'Don't you want children?'

'Of course,' he said, dropping a kiss on her tangled hair. 'But maybe not quite so soon.'

'Well,' she said. 'Only time will tell.' She paused. 'Whatever is your mother going to say?'

His grin was lazy. 'If she arrives at this minute—a great deal.'

'But she told me about the prophesy—that a fair-haired foreigner would cause the end of the House of the Wolf.'

'But that has already happened, my sweet one. Now it is the House of Summer that awaits my summer bride.'

'Why, yes,' she said. 'So, it is. I—I'd forgotten that. But I still don't think your mother's going to be very happy about the situation. I knew she disapproved of me being with you at Portofino.'

'She was concerned,' he said. 'Because she knew I had fallen irrevocably in love with a girl who belonged to another man, and that if I could not have her as my wife, I would never marry, and there would be no heir to carry on the Valieri name. That grieved her for my stepfather's sake.'

He kissed her again. 'But what she will tell you when we all meet tomorrow, is that she intends to sing in public again—and the first time will be at our wedding.'

'Oh.' Maddie choked a little. 'Oh—that would be so wonderful.'

'And I have no doubt,' he added in a resigned tone, 'that she will wish to take you shopping.'

For a moment, she saw herself reflected again in a swirl of wild silk. Found she was visualising the aisle of a church, and seeing Andrea turning from the altar to watch her walk towards him, the passion in his gaze mingled with reverence. The man she loved, waiting with love.

'But not for a dress,' she said dreamily. 'Because I already have the perfect one. All it needs is one last stitch.'

And she raised her smiling mouth for his kiss.

* * * * *

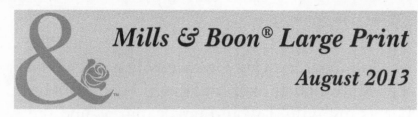

Mills & Boon® Large Print
August 2013

MASTER OF HER VIRTUE
Miranda Lee

THE COST OF HER INNOCENCE
Jacqueline Baird

A TASTE OF THE FORBIDDEN
Carole Mortimer

COUNT VALIERI'S PRISONER
Sara Craven

THE MERCILESS TRAVIS WILDE
Sandra Marton

A GAME WITH ONE WINNER
Lynn Raye Harris

HEIR TO A DESERT LEGACY
Maisey Yates

SPARKS FLY WITH THE BILLIONAIRE
Marion Lennox

A DADDY FOR HER SONS
Raye Morgan

ALONG CAME TWINS...
Rebecca Winters

AN ACCIDENTAL FAMILY
Ami Weaver

0713 Rom LP

Mills & Boon® Large Print
September 2013

A RICH MAN'S WHIM
Lynne Graham

A PRICE WORTH PAYING?
Trish Morey

A TOUCH OF NOTORIETY
Carole Mortimer

THE SECRET CASELLA BABY
Cathy Williams

MAID FOR MONTERO
Kim Lawrence

CAPTIVE IN HIS CASTLE
Chantelle Shaw

HEIR TO A DARK INHERITANCE
Maisey Yates

ANYTHING BUT VANILLA...
Liz Fielding

A FATHER FOR HER TRIPLETS
Susan Meier

SECOND CHANCE WITH THE REBEL
Cara Colter

FIRST COMES BABY...
Michelle Douglas

om LP

ML

9-13